For F

With Best Wishes

from

Mike + me,

John Raushenbush

Dec. 2018

Edited by Marlene Blessing
Cover Illustration: David Michael Beck
Cover Design: HR Dowling

1

The second book of Yellowstone tales is once again dedicated to our eight grandchildren—Graham, Kailie, Brice, Grace, Jake, John, Sam & Paige—for whom all the stories were originally written.

Preface by Art Davidson

Spinoza, Einstein, and *The Secret of the Magic Berries*

If they were with us today and had young ones about the house, boy, would Spinoza and Einstein ever love to read these stories to their children. Each in his way has spoken of our need to know the Mike Mulligans of this world—and to find *The Secret of the Magic Berries*.

"The highest end to which humans could aspire," said Spinoza in words that could have been a little easier for children to understand, "consists in the knowledge of the union existing between the mind and the whole of nature."

Einstein put it this way: "Our task must be to embrace all living creatures and the whole of nature and its beauty . . . to focus our attention on the wonders and realities of the universe around us."

Storyteller John Raushenbush takes us on an enchanting journey that is full of such wonders and realities. Nick and Geni, now 14 and growing fonder of each other by the day, set out to explore the wilds of Yellowstone together. Guided by the magic eagle they call Mike Mulligan, their "eyes and ears focus on the world around them."

As they venture deep into the forest, the teens have an eerie feeling that something is following them. The premonition grows stronger. They would "take a step, stop, and look around hoping to discover whatever it was . . . The creature, trying to take one more stealthy step before coming to a halt, had crept a little closer."

Closer and closer the wild animals come . . . and they to them. Until, with the help of their eagle friend, Mike Mulligan, Nick and Geni enter the world of these wild beings in a most amazing way.

"Nick lifted the mysterious branch out of his backpack,

plucked two berries [the eagle had brought] for the teens to gulp down together. Slowly but steadily, the changes began to take shape . . . Geni's reaction was total astonishment. Sensing the changes, she touched her new gray-brown coat, tufted ears, black-tipped tail, and of all things, a gorgeous display of whiskers.

"Accustomed to morphing into wild creatures, Nick waited calmly as dense dark fur, white hair on his throat and chest, a silvery face, and thick, full tail replaced the body of this 14 year-old boy."

Suddenly, they are not just ever-so-close to wildlife. They become wild creatures themselves!

Squirrels, owls, wolves, and wolverines. Beavers, bear, moose, and mountain lions. They all wander through these stories. And we wander with them, suspending, for a while, the notion that we live in one world, and they in another. Through Nick and Geni, who may shapeshift into a bear or wolf one moment and a bird soaring above the trees the next, we go deep into the very being of wild birds and animals.

Whether showing a beaver build a dam or a mother wolf looking for a lost pup, these stories have a way of reminding us of our own special moments in nature, our own encounters with a bear, or a moose, or a flock of swans taking flight. And we are reminded that, for all the distractions of modern life, we, too, are creatures of nature.

These stories are fun, full of surprises, and a whole lot easier for young minds to embrace than the philosophy of Spinoza. They take us out there with the wolves and elk. And if we listen carefully, we'll hear them calling to something deep within us.

Mike Mulligan and the Secret of the Magic Berries is a joy to read. The adventures of Nick and Geni in Yellowstone are an even greater joy to share with children and grandchildren. It's important for young people to hear stories that bring them into the natural world and help them expand their sense of who they are and how they can share this world with other living creatures.

Mike Mulligan
and the Secret of the Magic Berries

By John Raushenbush

Contents

The Birdcage Mystery

Chapter 1—The Injured Birds Attack

Once outside, he peered at the threesome staring back at him, squinted toward the bright light, and took off at great speed into the night. In an instant he was gone . . . . *but not before they saw who it was.*

****

The second summer in Yellowstone Park quickly proved to be as exciting for Nick and Geni, now 14 year-olds, as the first summer had been. They had stayed in touch by text and email during the winter months. Occasionally, Geni lapsed into her native language if only to see how Nick was advancing in Spanish II. As March melted into April, the friends shared an eagerness for May, knowing that both of their families planned to return to the park as soon as the school year was over. The two couldn't wait!

In addition to the remarkable friendship the teens shared with Mike Mulligan, a bald eagle Nick had saved from a coyote attack, only the boy knew the secret of the magic berries, at least so far. Geni was not yet aware that the berries, the eagle's gift to Nick, had the power to change a person for a day into one of Yellowstone's fascinating wild creatures.

Soon after Nick came back to the park, Geni arrived with her family. After she had settled into her cabin, the pair went hiking through the forest, pleased that it was a warm and sunny late spring day. Eyes and ears focused on the world around, the friends were sure that a new and intriguing adventure would add some spice to summertime in the park. Little did they know that the experience they were about to have was to be one of the most exciting . . . ever. But first, as usual, little things tended to crop up before the big ones.

The earliest he knew something was wrong was when Nick overheard one of the park rangers, Gary Heathmore, talking to his dad outside the Canyon Village general store.

"Yessir," the ranger was saying, "three nights during the past week something has broken into the cages where we keep the injured birds. Killed two, a red-tailed hawk and a ruffed grouse, and injured an American kestrel."

"That's really disturbing," his dad replied. "The ruffed grouse's distinctive habit of beating its wings against a log makes it the drummer-musician of the forest. Any idea what's doing it?"

"Odd thing," Ranger Heathmore went on, "the birds weren't eaten, only tossed around and chewed on. Can't imagine that a hungry wolf or coyote would leave anything but the feathers."

"So what are you going to do about it?" was Dad's next question.

"Well, tonight I plan to sit near the cages in my truck with a spotlight and a dart gun on the seat next to me. With any luck, if the culprit returns, I'll be able to dart it."

When the ranger climbed into his truck, Kiska, his handsome husky, jumped in behind and off they went. As they were driving home, Nick's dad commented that he was just as puzzled as the ranger. "I can understand it when a starving animal breaks into a place despite the people smells—but not the way it happened this time. This creature clearly wasn't lacking for food."

"What could have done it?" Nick wondered. "And what will the rangers do if the critter comes again?"

"You heard Gary," Dad said. "If he can, he'll dart it and then decide what to do."

"But, Dad, how far will he go?" The boy had come to love the wildlife in Yellowstone so much that he couldn't imagine harming one, even to protect the birds.

"I guess that depends on what kind of animal the attacker is," his father explained. "Some more dangerous ones he'd have to get rid of; but most I imagine he'd be able to relocate in the park. Still, many animals will return to their home territory, no matter how far away you take them. And when you think about those that come back, I can only guess that if they broke into the bird cages once, they're more likely to do it again."

Nick's question had been answered, but it didn't make him feel any better. Ranger Heathmore seemed to suspect a wolf, although he had added that it could have been any number of predators. He mentioned that it could even have been a raptor, explaining that birds of prey will on occasion attack each other. The ranger's suspicions particularly troubled Nick for two reasons—first because wolves were his favorite park animals; second, because they usually found the way back to their packs, no matter how far they were removed.

Still unsettled when he went to bed, Nick lay awake wondering how Ranger Heathmore, on guard duty all night, was getting along up at the "Animal Hospital" (as the park personnel called the birdcages lined up inside the fence). He must have fallen asleep because the next thing he knew, a glimmer of first light was filtering through the trees outside his window. He jumped into his clothes and sprinted to the kitchen to see if Mom or Dad had any news. Then he stopped, listened, and looked around.

No one was there.

Nick glanced at the clock on the counter and immediately felt rather stupid. It was only 5:15 a.m. He tiptoed over to his parents' room, but before he was even close to the door he could hear his father snoring peacefully. What now?

Back to the kitchen he went, wondering if a bowl of cereal might help him come up with a plan—and perhaps it did. He decided to leave a note for his parents, pick up Geni, and walk over to the ranger station where surely someone would know if another bird had been attacked. It wasn't too far, and anyway early morning in Yellowstone was his favorite time. It was impossible to go anywhere at dawn without coming upon something interesting.

Along the way, Nick repeated all the details he knew to Geni, who immediately asked, "What's a husky? And also, what did the ranger mean when he said he would *dart the animal?*"

From time to time the boy was reminded that Geni had been in the U.S. only a year. Although she had lived much of her life in Europe and had a broader familiarity with the world, she still needed help from him with certain expressions and ideas that he took for granted.

"Ranger Heathmore's dog, Kiska, a husky, was with him the morning we learned about the bird attacks. Huskies are a favorite dog breed in Alaska," he explained, "because they love the cold and are strong and tough enough to pull sleds. In lots of remote parts of

Alaska, people use dogsleds with teams of huskies for transportation. There are also sled dog races."

"I would like to try a dogsled some winter," Geni remarked.

"As for your second question, when you dart an animal, it means you are putting it to sleep for a short time so you can help it in some way. For example, you can move it to a new place or fix an injury if you need to. Depending on the type of animal, the one assaulting the birds will have to be darted and removed."

The teens took the path through an aspen grove, then into a clearing that looked out across the river, and up onto steep rocky cliffs that jutted way out above the valley. It was an ideal spot, partly because Nick often caught glimpses of mountain goats foraging in the green meadows, white flecks against the gray rocks, clinging precariously to the cliffs.

Pausing to take out the binoculars he always carried in his backpack, the boy scanned the riverbanks, zeroing in on a familiar bald eagle sitting on the branch of a dead tree as he waited for fish to rise to an early morning insect hatch.

Mike Mulligan flew down and landed on Nick's shoulder as he often did. "What are you two up to this a.m.," he inquired. "Did you plan your arrival in time to share my trout breakfast?"

"Exactly where is this *pedazo de pescado*, this fish morsel, you are referring to?" Geni wondered. "Are you hiding it from us somewhere? Or is it only in your imagination?"

"Just a matter of time," the eagle replied, slightly miffed that she had questioned his fishing expertise. And with that he was gone, swooping down and gliding along the surface of the stream before he disappeared in the distance.

"I wonder whether birds, injured or not, have a place in his diet," Nick posed. Quietly continuing, he realized that his concern was nonsense. "No, for sure that eagle is too civilized to be a cannibal. Just ask him!"

"*Sin duda*, without a doubt, he prefers a plump trout or an occasional hamburger . . . raw!" Geni observed.

Chapter 2—The Cougar and the Mountain Goat

Looking out into the valley, they spotted the usual herd of bison, steam issuing from their nostrils as warm breath struck the cold air of dawn, and three bull elk grazing in a grassy pasture, one with a magnificent set of antlers. As he lifted his binocs toward the cliffs, Nick was excited to catch sight of a white dot ambling among the rocks.

"Look up there, Geni," he urged, handing her the binoculars, "those critters are so hard to see." Sure enough there was a baby mountain goat munching happily in the cliffside meadow.

"O, *es tan lindo*, it is so cute," she exclaimed. "What is it called?"

"It's called a *kid*, same as baby goats on farms and elsewhere."

"In Spanish it's *un cabrito*," she said.

Nick was about to turn away when the whole scene changed. In a flash of red, a ferruginous hawk, a mere speck soaring near the clouds, glided down to settle on a rocky overhang a short distance away. Then, a head popped up among the rocks and a fat marmot appeared, making its customary clicking noises to indicate that danger was nearby. An instant later, a movement near the little goat caught the boy's eye.

"Omigosh, Geni," Nick raised his voice a notch, "look toward the rocks behind the little guy!"

The teen twosome could hardly believe their eyes. What, moments earlier, had drawn the hawk speedily to the cliffs and alerted the marmot in its burrow, was suddenly unmistakable. A mountain lion, crawling silently on its belly closer and closer to the goat, was almost ready to pounce.

Hearing the marmot's shrill warning, the kid leapt from the grass patch onto the side of a boulder a few feet away and scrambled nimbly onto the top. The lion was after it in a split second. But luckily for the wee one, the wild cat, though agile, didn't have the gripping hooves or rock-climbing skill that goats have. Yet on it came, clawing at the smooth side of the boulder while the kid, suddenly frozen in place, was too frightened to budge.

Just as the lion was about to reach the top, there was another movement from behind the boulder and out charged a huge ram, one of the biggest goats Nick had ever seen. Lowering its great head and horns, it butted the lion with force enough to hurl it off the ledge, and send it tumbling down onto the rocks some 15 to 20 feet below. It lay there for a moment, stunned, then picked itself up and headed off in the opposite direction to look elsewhere for a less strenuous breakfast opportunity. It never even glanced back at the two goats.

The two human members of the curious group of onlookers let out a cheer as they watched the ram and kid disappear up over the rock face. Nick and Geni had to pinch themselves to be sure they hadn't dreamt the whole thing.

Then all four of the spectators gazed at the lion disappearing behind a boulder and a row of jagged spires. The hawk turned a pair of sharp eyes briefly toward the marmot who clicked again and hastily scurried into its lair. The raptor rose majestically off the cliffside and hovered above the landscape for a moment before he caught an updraft and soared away.

Nick and Geni watched the beautiful bird, often mistaken for a bald eagle because of its light gray head, snowy breast, and the white underside of tail-feathers. The largest of North American hawks, it got its name, *ferruginous,* from rusty colored wings and feathered legs. As it wheeled ever higher, they heard its cry, *geeeer, geeeer,* becoming faint in the distance.

"There's a bird call I bet you've never heard before," Nick remarked.

"Geeeer, geeeer," Geni imitated. Then, a little perplexed, she wondered, "Isn't it natural for predators like lions or wolves to go after other animals for food? How else can they survive?"

"Yes, you're right," Nick agreed, "but it still makes you feel good when the cute little fella avoids becoming a snack for the powerful big guy. What's more, that cougar is a great hunter—it will not go hungry for long."

Continuing to the ranger station, they were relieved to see Ranger Heathmore's truck in the parking area. They went inside and found him in the office drinking a cup of coffee.

"You two certainly got off to an early start today," he smiled.

"We were still worrying about the injured birds when we woke up, so we decided to hike on over to find out if anything occurred last night."

"No activity," he answered. "I kept an eye on the area until just before dawn, then double-checked each of the cages before I left. Guess I'll wait a few days, then try again."

Unfortunately, all of them soon learned that waiting a few days would prove to be too long. The very next night the intruder sneaked in and attacked an osprey with a broken wing. This time the entire ranger station was up in arms. Everyone volunteered to stand watch so that the cages would be guarded every night until the midnight marauder was caught.

Even Nick's father offered to take a turn and, of course, the boy stated emphatically that he and Geni would keep him company. Knowing how miserable Nick was about this whole business, especially the possibility that the marauder was a wolf, he tousled his son's hair and said, "I'll be glad to have you both with me."

Among the cluster of family and friends close to the teenagers, only Mike Mulligan paid minimal attention to the fate of the injured osprey. "As I've mentioned before, there are too many of those birds in the park; they think they own the rights to the best fishing; and they build nests too lousy for any other bird ever to occupy. So I can't get too worked up." His complaints emphasized the well-known fact that *there was no love lost* between these two raptors.

It was several days before Nick's dad learned that their turn for sentry duty had come. In the meantime, Nick and Geni had hiked out into the Lamar Valley to look for the Lamar Canyon wolf pack that lived there, one of the largest in the park. They came upon the pack fairly quickly, spotting them down where Pebble Creek flowed into the big river that snaked through the valley. Seeing the pack always brought to Nick's mind the thrilling day he had spent among them as a wolf pup. He counted fifteen or so, the adults lying drowsily in the sun, the one-year-olds pawing each other as they playfully leapt into the air. Even the new-born pups were staggering around bumping into things and suckling breakfast from their mothers. It made the twosome feel good to see them behaving so normally.

16

"So maybe it wasn't a wolf after all," Geni offered, knowing that the sight of the pack would make Nick wonder. "It could have been a bobcat, a lynx, or especially a coyote, couldn't it?"

"Yes it could," Nick agreed, still puzzled that the birds hadn't been eaten.

Later that afternoon, Dad and the teens prepared for the all-night adventure, Dad by snoring on his bed and Nick, too wound up to nap, by reading several chapters in Terhune's marvelous book about a collie named *Lad*. Somewhat reluctantly, Geni helped Mom make a sack of tuna sandwiches and a thermos of hot chocolate as she mumbled something about "the importance of learning to prepare one's own food." But when Nick offered to help, her snarl quickly convinced him that he had better back off. However, he did pack the car with warm clothing and flashlights, along with a special park mobile to alert the ranger station in case there was anything to report.

Chapter 3—The Midnight Watch

As they pulled up near the birdcages, Nick's dad and the teens walked around the enclosures to learn which ones were occupied and needed to be watched. The injured American kestrel was still there; it had been joined recently by a red-tailed hawk and by the largest owl in existence, a great gray owl that has been described as "a dapper fellow dressed in a gray suit with a bow tie across its neck and a surprised look on its face."

While they were studying the area, Ranger Heathmore drove up as expected and approached them to provide instructions, Kiska at his side. "I plan to sleep in my clothes on the cot in the office," he said, "so if the prowler returns, just call me. I can be here in three minutes to track it down. And above all, don't yell at it, don't approach it, and especially don't chase it . . . *just call me!*"

"Don't worry," Dad assured him. "We're certainly not nutty enough to take on the predator—be it a wolf, a weasel, or a bushy-tailed woodrat—with our only weapon, a thermos of hot chocolate."

"I'm still puzzled that the birds weren't eaten," the ranger continued, mirroring Nick's thoughts. "That aspect of the whole business is really odd. Anyway, I've brought a flashlight with a mighty beam for you—it may scare off the intruder, but all you need to do is identify it. If I get here fast enough, I'll be able to track it, even at night, so be sure to call me pronto!" And he was gone.

The surveillance team sat in the truck watching the skies grow darker and darker. Nothing was moving, not even the birds. When the teens were unable to keep their eyes open any longer, Dad suggested that they take a snooze, promising to wake them if an uninvited guest appeared. The next thing they knew, he was calling softly and holding out two cups of cocoa.

"It's 2 a.m.," he said. "If anything is going to happen, I think it will be soon."

They took a sip or two, ate a sandwich, and peered out toward the cages, hoping to catch a glimpse of something moving, or even flashes of light among the night shadows. Finding the scene both eerie and exciting, Nick quickly lost interest in food and drink.

Then, without warning, Dad grabbed Nick's arm and whispered sharply, "Don't make a sound! But look over at the chain-link gate. Can you make out something scratching and digging around it?"

Nick jabbed Geni with his elbow and together they stared toward the cages, straining to catch sight of whatever Dad thought he had spotted. Although they could see nothing, they began to hear a scratching noise. But more than that, there was a commotion of flapping wings and bird cries from inside the cages that grew louder and louder.

All three watchers jumped out of the truck and in the next moment Nick's father pointed the flashlight in the direction of the sounds. And there it was! The beam flashed on an animal digging a hole under the fence. When the light struck him, he stopped digging and started to scramble back out. Once outside, he peered at the threesome staring back at him, squinted toward the bright light, and took off at great speed into the night. In an instant he was gone . . . *but not before they saw who it was.*

There, in the beam, looking tremendously guilty as only a dog can look, was Kiska, Ranger Heathmore's husky.

Nick stared at Dad, he stared back at Nick, then both stared at Geni, all three of them too astonished and disturbed to speak. With the saddest expression on his face, Dad murmured softly, "What we have just seen is absolutely awful. It will make Gary totally heartbroken."

"Are you going to call him now?" Nick asked.

"No," he answered, "I'm going to drop you two off at the cabins and then drive over to the ranger station. I need to deliver the bad news right away and in person."

"What will happen to Kiska?" Geni asked.

"That's something I'd rather not try to predict," was his reply.

Weeks went by and they didn't hear anything more about Kiska. They only knew that the dog was nowhere to be seen. Nor did Nick have the heart to ask Ranger Heathmore about the husky when he bumped into him outside the Canyon Village general store. However, the boy must have hassled his father about Kiska's fate too often because finally he told his son, "Hang in there, you'll be the first to know when there is *anything* to know."

Then one day toward the end of June, Dad burst into the house with a grin on his face that signaled he had something important to tell them, something that was good news. Nick and his mom could hardly hide their eagerness to hear what it was.

"I just ran into Gary in the village," he said, "and guess what he told me?" (Dad was too impatient to reveal what the ranger had said to delay for guessing.) "After discovering Kiska's attacks on the injured birds, he contacted a family he knew in Fairbanks, Alaska, who train sled dogs. He asked them if they'd be willing to take the husky, despite what he had done. And can you believe it, they said they would."

In fact, just this morning the family had called Gary to report not only all of this, but also another important detail that made his father grin more broadly than ever. Nick listened eagerly to the second news flash that he couldn't wait to share with Geni and Mike Mulligan.

"But hold on," Dad yelled after him—"there's even more. As a reward for our help in solving the birdcage mystery, you, Geni, and I can each keep for dinner one trout that we catch in Slough Creek, or anywhere—and since you're the better fisherman, I'll give you mine."

As Nick flew out the door, he shouted back to his parents, "Wow! That's a happy ending."

"A happy ending? I like those," said the handsome bald eagle as he landed on the boy's shoulder. "Tell me about it."

"Wait till we meet Geni," Nick shot back. "Then I'll tell you both the good news."

A few minutes later, sitting together on Geni's porch, Nick shared the entire story and its special ending with his buddies. "Ranger Heathmore asked friends in Fairbanks, Alaska," he repeated, "to adopt Kiska. The ranger had also wondered," he went on, "if the husky might be trained as a sled dog."

21

"When Dad saw the ranger this morning he learned the best news of all—Kiska was quickly becoming *el numero uno* sled dog on the team!"

Mister Moose

Chapter 4—Nick to the Rescue

The morning after Geni returned from a family visit to friends in Bozeman, she and Nick decided the day was perfect for a picnic. Nick kept silent about one of the reasons he was so eager for her to return. Now, as they prepared to hike to the Firehole River, he was waiting for *just the right moment* to relate the remarkable adventure that happened while she was gone.

Together, Nick and Geni collected the picnic ingredients, with the exception of one item in particular. The missing ingredient from the picnic menu was the main dish itself, a lip-smacking, fresh-out-of-the-water trout to share, cleaned and cooked to perfection on a built-for-the-occasion stream-side grill. They loaded their backpacks with the food, plus a grate for the campfire, while they chatted about how and where to spend the next few hours.

Once the decision was made—to include both a fly-fishing competition and a swimming opportunity—Nick added wading sneakers and his yard-sale vest to the pack, while Geni folded in her jazzy *Reel Gals* outfit, now a year old. They wore swimsuits under their clothes and headed off, fly-rods in hand, knowing that the Firehole was the best place in the park for both fishing and swimming.

The two were excited about the fishing competition, a test of skill against each other. The winner would be awarded not only the KitKats stashed in the backpack, but even better would feel the exhilaration of earning the title, *Angler-of-the-Day*. As best friends, the two continued to enjoy the friendly rivalry that began in the Lamar River the day they met.

After they finalized the plan, Geni paused to remark, "*Un momento*. I thought it was illegal to keep a trout caught in the park waters." The pair normally believed in and followed this rule *to the letter*.

"I've kept it a secret to surprise you," Nick replied. "The rangers told my dad each of us could keep a fish as a reward for helping solve the mystery of Kiska and the injured birds."

"Now that we've heard the fish tale," said a voice from above belonging to none other than Mike Mulligan as he landed a few feet away on a low tree stump, "got any new ones?"

As they walked along, the eagle glided serenely overhead. Nick couldn't contain himself any longer. He turned to Geni, eyes twinkling, and asked, "Have you ever seen a moose really up close?"

"Only far off," she answered, recalling the one, standing in the river, that she was painting a year ago when all the mountain lion excitement occurred. "It looked big and dark with a long face kind of like a horse."

"You got it," he said. "Moose are among the largest animals in North America. It just so happens that I've also been in a rush to tell you about not one but two amazing moose adventures that occurred near here when you were away."

"Do I have any choice?" she wondered.

"Well, it happens to be a very special moose tale, as you will soon agree."

"Maybe another time," the eagle groaned as he lifted off. "Time is food; food is time. I'll be back when your lunch is on the grill, and mine is . . . well, we'll have to wait and see."

"I guess that leaves the story for me," Geni concluded, "or me for the story, so *¡vamos!*, just go for it!"

Unfazed by his buddies' lack of enthusiasm, Nick began his tale.

Nick had gone out for a bike ride shortly after sunrise. As usual, he prepared his backpack with a rain poncho, binoculars, a water bottle, a few snacks, and his Swiss army knife. It was a beautiful day in the park, full of sunshine, blue skies, and the musty smell of early morning dew on the leaves and plants.

I had no particular plan in mind, but I thought I'd look for bison or elk where they often grazed alongside the Madison River several miles from our cabin. Sure enough, I spotted a small herd of bison munching a grassy breakfast on the hillside below one of my favorite lookout points. I stopped to watch these great shaggy beasts, especially the comical calves, romping around, tripping over clumps of grass, often bumping into each other. I pulled out my binoculars, scanned the entire valley, and caught a glimpse of a bald eagle perched on the limb of a dead tree at the edge of the river.

Pausing to see if Geni was still paying attention, Nick quizzed, "What can you tell me about bald eagles?"

"It is the national bird for your country," she responded, "sometimes appearing on coins and stamps. Often he can be seen trying to avoid listening to a certain boy tell stories about his adventures in the park."

"Right you are again, though I fear you know too much about a certain raptor and a certain boy. But back to the amazing moose— you just might be more impressed by the time the plot ends!"

I left my bike and the bison herd, hiked over a little rise and down into the woods. I followed what looked like a deer or antelope trail and was just about to head back when I heard a strange noise. It was a rasping, clacking noise as if two hard surfaces were scraping or whacking against each other.

As the racket grew louder, I listened for a moment or two. The closer I got, the more I heard other noises, including rustles, thumps, and crunches. I wondered what in the world was making such a ruckus?

And then, when I saw what it was, I was stunned. There in a thick grove of trees and shrubs was the biggest if not also the handsomest Bull Moose I had ever seen. I was close enough to notice sweat glistening on his flanks and a worried look in his eyes. It was obvious that he was in a bit of trouble.

Somehow, his huge antlers had gotten caught in the branches of an Aspen tree—perhaps they had tangled when he was scratching himself or chewing the bark. However it had happened, he was firmly caught. The more he struggled to free himself, the more wiped out he became. As he grew weaker, the more frightened and helpless he must have felt. He had beaten down all the bushes around the tree during his struggle, opening up a circle of bare earth where once there had been ferns, shrubs, and tall grasses. In trying to free himself, he had snapped off the tip of an antler, leaving it shaped like a W.

After a few minutes, I slipped off my backpack, set it on the ground, removed the Swiss army knife and put it in my pants pocket. As I walked toward the miserable moose, I spoke softly hoping he would let me come nearer without becoming even more agitated.

26

"Don't be afraid, Moose-kin," I said quietly. "I'm going to do my best to help you. Just relax and let me try to set you free."

At first, hearing my voice, he tried frantically to shake himself loose. But it seemed that he somehow figured out the more he shook the tighter he was trapped. Finally, he became still and watched me.

As I stood next to the aspen, I saw what I needed to do. I climbed up the trunk of the tree and crept out on the limb that trapped the moose. Once there, I pulled the knife from my pocket, opened the saw blade, and began to cut through the branches that gripped his antlers. It took about ten minutes to cut him loose, but soon he was free.

"There you go," I said, catching my breath after my sawing, "but don't get too frisky or you'll knock me out of this tree."

He stretched his neck, shook his entire body, looked around and peered up at me. I was happy to see normal brightness back in his eyes. Then he turned and started to walk calmly away. At the edge of the clearing, he stopped and looked at me again—I was still out on the limb. He nodded, which I think was his way of saying, "I understand what you've just done for me." Of course, I'll never be sure. In any case, I would meet him again soon.

"Es increíble," Geni exclaimed, "and you actually saw him again?"

"Yes, I really did, but the second time was very different."

Chapter 5—The Gold Bracelet

After hearing Nick's first moose story, Geni was definitely more interested and eager to learn more. So Nick continued to recount his next moose adventure.

Only a couple of days later, I was out exploring, this time along the Firehole River. I had gone there once with Mom and Dad, to a spot where we waded into the water, then swam to the deep part and let the current rush us swiftly downstream. We used our hands and feet to keep from crashing into the huge boulders and smooth walls of the gorge and sped along until the river slowed and widened. After an awesome ride, we would wade out, hike back up, and do it again.

To get to that place was quite a hike, and I knew better than to swim alone—at least I thought I did.

I wandered along the bank, jumping from boulder to boulder and tossing little pebbles at targets drifting by in the river. Suddenly, I noticed something trapped in the split ends of a broken tree branch jammed into a crack in the rock wall. It had caught my eye because it looked so out-of-place, a sparkling golden circle eye-catching against the deep blue color of the Firehole.

The more I stared at it, the more I wanted to retrieve it from the stream. I leapt over to a boulder just above the branch, got down on my hands and knees, and started to crawl toward the water. When I arrived at the edge of the bank, I lay on my stomach and reached out toward the shiny thing. I stretched as far as I could, but I couldn't quite touch it. I made one final lunge then grabbed the golden object just as I fell off the rock and down into the rushing water.

"As I rose to the surface," Nick looked at his friend, "I realized that I was caught in a current that was much stronger than any I had ever faced. It swept me downstream so powerfully that I couldn't control which way I went—frontward or backward, head first or feet first."

"Were you scared?" Geni interrupted.

"You bet! I was scared stiff," Nick answered, "and quickly starting to get cold too."

"So what happened next?" she asked, actually appearing a little anxious.

There I was shooting along with no control over speed and no control over direction either. In fact, I was pretty helpless. Suddenly, the Firehole took a sharp turn between two large boulders, the water churning wildly. Feet first, I bounced off the flat side of the upstream rock, felt myself spinning around and, wham!, saw stars as I thumped against a smooth log lodged in a crack in the rock wall.

After a short time, I was floating slowly in calmer water. I opened one eye and there, much to my amazement, was a large dark figure sporting a magnificent set of antlers. I blinked, struggled to open the other eye, and finally realized that the antlers were being lowered down to the water inches in front of me.

Instinctively, I grabbed the antlers and held on tight, only to be lifted into the air and set down gently atop the large dark shape. I was still in the middle of the stream, but to my surprise I was out of the water and parked comfortably on the back of an animal. An animal?! A moose. My Moose! It was more than my waterlogged brain could comprehend at first, but as the fuzziness faded and my vision returned, I could see I was hanging on for dear life to a broken moose antler shaped like a W!

Mister Moose turned around in the stream and headed for shore. While I held on tight, he scrambled up the bank and on into the woods until we came to a clearing near where I had fallen in. He turned his head and looked around at me

29

with an expression that seemed to suggest it was time for me to climb down. No sooner had I jumped off than he started to fade into the forest. Before he disappeared, however, he looked back at me and, once again giving me that same little nod, this time as if to say, "Now we are even." But I'll never be absolutely sure.

When I found my pack lying on the ground, I started to feel even better. Now cold and hungry, I put on the poncho and ate my snack. Soon I was pretty much back to normal, but still shaken.

As I started walking home, I felt something in my soggy pants pocket. When I reached in, I pulled out a shiny gold bracelet. It was just as eye-catching as it had been when I first spotted it. Back at home, my mother took one look at me and asked, "Where in the world have you been and why do you look scraped, rumpled, and waterlogged?"

"You wouldn't believe me if I told you," I replied, "but I do have something special for you."

I pulled the bracelet out of my pocket and handed it to her. As she slipped it on her wrist, she smiled, "It's lovely. I like it a lot! And before bedtime you will tell me how you found it." Later, while she sat on my bed, I told her the whole incredible story.

Nick's mother shuddered visibly, opened her mouth twice, but no sound came out until finally, "I assume you learned an enormous lesson the hard way today, so I don't need to say anything more."

Geni was also at a loss for words until they reached the Firehole River and sat down on the rocks to get lunch ready. Then she looked at her friend and stated quietly, "You had quite the adventure while I was up in Bozeman, didn't you? I feel lucky you are here and okay."

Not wanting to get into a discussion of such a tricky subject as *luck*, and having learned early on that she could be distracted by the hint of food, Nick opened his backpack, put on his fishing vest and sneakers, and began to rig his rod and reel.

"Lunch is going to be mighty sparse if one of us doesn't hook into a two-pounder."

Chapter 6—Casting for Lunch

Geni scrambled into her fishing outfit, grabbed her rod, and clomped off clumsily in her heavyweight boots. "If you cast a fly onto that water before I'm ready, I will cast a spell over you, causing fish only to laugh at your fly, and that's for sure!" she said emphatically.

Although the teens teased each other about it, they loved their fly-fishing competition and took it quite seriously. Aware that Nick was more practiced and skillful, though she would never admit it to him, not today, not ever—*ni hoy, ni nunca*—Geni tried to learn something from him every time they fished. He was well aware how much she had improved since their first summer together.

"What fly are you using?" Nick asked.

"A tiny Parachute Adams, size 18," came her answer.

Nick smiled to himself over her perfect choice. "That's a good one," was his only comment.

Nick waded into the Firehole a short distance upstream from Geni, leaving her a riffle in which, he was certain, there would be rainbows. As for himself, the boy concentrated on several pools beneath the rock walls across the stream. In these deep holes, he knew, hungry brown trout would lurk, waiting for an insect to float gently by.

Although they were too far apart to keep an eye on each other's activity, Nick was pretty sure that Geni, still learning the technique of rapid fly switching, would continue using the Adams. Nick, on the other hand, started with an Elk Hair Caddis, soon moved on to a Light Cahill, finally deciding that a small Blue-Winged Olive might prove to be the fly of the day.

His cast dropped the olive, without a splash, eight inches from the bank along the far side of the stream. In ten seconds or less, there was a flash from deep in the pool, followed by the unmistakable ripple of a fish breaking the surface, and then a jerk on the line as the brown gobbled the fly.

"Got one," he shouted downstream.

"Got one," the echo came back at him.

"Hold on," Nick exclaimed, immediately puzzled, "that was no echo."

"Didn't you hear me," came the echo voice again, "are you deaf? I said, 'got one!'" And there was Geni proudly holding a nice rainbow high over her head.

The two fishermen climbed onto the bank and, carrying their prizes, met near the tree where they had stashed their backpacks.

"*¿Es grande?*" Geni was the first to ask. "How big is it?"

"An inch bigger than yours," was Nick's confident reply.

"Bobo! Anyone can see yours is *minúsculo*."

"What is obviously required at a critical moment like this," declared a handsome bald eagle, settling once again on the branch next to the backpack, "is a totally trustworthy and impartial referee. And I happen to know pre-cisely the right one. Moreover, the fee for

33

services rendered—very reasonable, I assure you—shall be . . . um . . . yes . . . shall be either a rainbow or maybe a brown trout, fresh out of the water."

Nick looked at Geni; Geni looked at Nick. Both clapped a hand over their mouths and then, when they couldn't stand it any longer, burst into great peals of laughter.

"I would have thought that such a generous offer might be taken more seriously," the raptor observed, as he strained, in vain, not to laugh with them.

Still chuckling, Nick took the brown trout down to the edge of the stream, where he cleaned and rinsed it in a shallow pool. Then, after arranging a dozen smooth river rocks to make a temporary grill in their picnic spot, he grabbed his backpack to retrieve the grate. First, he lit a match to a pile of sticks he had arranged in the firepit. He then rubbed a little oil on the skin of the brown, flicked a dash of salt and pepper inside and a splash of lemon juice inside and out before setting the fish on the grate. The rainbow, however, he left untouched.

Mike Mulligan breathed a sigh of relief when he saw that the rainbow Nick handed to him had not become the victim of human food preparation. "It just doesn't taste normal," the eagle explained, "when you mess with the flavor and blacken the skin.

Soon, sizzling softly on the fire, Nick's trout turned golden brown. He divided it into equal parts while Geni produced paper plates from her pack, each plate crowded with rolls, raw carrots, pickles, chips, and a hard-cooked egg. (The boy still couldn't figure out how anyone so petite and trim could have such a massive appetite.) For the dessert course, without the slightest squabble, they shared the KitKats, the prize for the winning fisherman.

After he devoured his rainbow, Mike sniffed at the rapidly shrinking mound of sweets, warning the pair that sometime he might have to try one. "Mother Eagle advised me against letting dessert spoil the main course so, though tempting, it won't be on my menu today."

When she had finished licking her lips, Geni turned to Nick, "I must admit, that despite the fact you're a guy, you are an excellent streamside chef."

As soon as the teens had stuffed the remains of the picnic into the backpacks, Nick asked Geni if she was ready for a swim. Neither one was allowed to go into the park streams alone. However, knowing they were both good swimmers, their parents gave them permission to swim together. This lazy stretch of the Firehole, unlike the spot where he had fallen in, was gentle enough and perfect for riding the river current.

"Last one in is a pasty-patch polecat," Nick shouted, as he dashed toward the river.

"*¿Qué es un pasty-patch polecat?*" he knew she would ask.

"*¡¡Es un comadreja de vientre amarillo!!*" the boy announced, pleased with himself for having waited patiently for the best moment to show off the Spanish phrase he had recently memorized.

"Yellow-bellied weasel!" she giggled. "*Tu español* has improved, I'll admit, but first I think I will drown you!"

35

"Yellow-bellied weasel?" Mike Mulligan cocked his head . "Sounds like it could be a delicacy."

The eagle perched on a tree limb to act as lifeguard while Nick and Geni dove into slow-moving water along the riverbank, then edged out into the faster flow in the middle. They were quickly swept downstream, brushing against rock walls smoothed by centuries of rushing water. They bobbed through the calm pools and tumbled over a series of dips and chutes, squealing with excitement while keeping a careful eye on each other.

After thirty minutes of sheer pleasure, the teens scrambled out onto a small beach where they sprawled in the warm sun to dry off. Señor Mulligan joined them, but only for a few minutes before announcing, "It's almost suppertime, so I'll be off in search of a *comadreja de vientre amarillo* or two," as he flapped twice and took flight.

As they enjoyed the warmth of the sand, Nick and Geni were startled by a loud crunching sound in the nearby trees. They jumped up and stared into the grove of aspen where, only thirty or forty feet away—they couldn't believe it—was a handsome bull moose gazing back at them.

"Geni," Nick exclaimed, "look at its right antler and tell me what you see?"

"*¡Extraordinario! ¡No lo creo!* I don't believe it!" was her astonished reply. "The antler is broken, and shaped like a W!"

As they headed for home, Geni, still curious about one thing in the moose tale, wanted to know, "Do you think your mom would show me the golden bracelet? I'd love to see it"

"She wears it every day," Nick responded, "and if you ask her I'm sure she'll be glad to show it to you."

The Weirdest Day . . . . EVER!

Chapter 7—The Eagle and His Buddy Stumble Upon the Unexpected

During their second summer in the park, Geni and her mom and dad decided to spend several days exploring Jackson, Wyoming, the historic western town, gateway to Jackson Hole and Grand Teton National Park. Before she left, Nick, who had visited there the previous summer, mentioned that the word "Hole" is used to describe the "high mountain valley" between the Gros Ventre and the rugged, spectacular Teton range.

"I'll be sure to share your geography lesson with my dad," Geni teased. "You and he have a lot of *teach-me* energy in common."

While she was away he knew he'd have to amuse himself, aside from any entertainment Mike Mulligan might provide. Little did he know, however, just how *amused* he would be!

The day after Geni left, Nick planned to get up before sunrise in order to be on Soda Butte Creek in time to take advantage of the early hatch. A hatch, he knew, was a bit like a chick coming out of its shell. Insects lay eggs which sink to the bottom of a stream. When the newborn bugs are ready, they rise to the surface and begin to fly. It can occur at different times during the day, but the *early hatch* is often the best. Hungry fish are waiting for it . . . and so are eager anglers, using flies that imitate the insects. He set his alarm, for 5a.m., turned off the light, and settled into a deep sleep.

After the alarm sounded, Nick was barely awake. He dressed in the dark, collected his fishing rod and tackle, and went off through the woods just as the first sunbeams were turning the night shadows into soft morning gold. This hour of the day was his favorite in Yellowstone, not only because it was beautiful, but because it was the time when strange and wonderful things always seemed to happen. Today would be no exception. He only wished that Geni were there to share whatever adventure he'd encounter.

The path that led Nick to the number-one fishing spot on the river (at least in his opinion) passed through a grove of aspen trees with a grassy clearing in the center. As he entered, he was surprised to hear tiny high-pitched voices, sounds he'd never heard before, barking out orders of some kind. There, in the middle of the meadow, was a gathering of rodents—rabbits, pikas (a little critter without a tail sometimes called a "rock rabbit"), red tree squirrels, and golden-mantled ground squirrels. Just as it became clear that they were engaged in some kind of animated entertainment, Mike Mulligan flew in and landed with a whoosh on the boy's shoulder.

"Wait till you see what's going on here," Nick whispered, turning toward his friend's ear, "but first promise that you won't gobble up any of the performers."

The eagle's head bobbed up and down, "Your memory is often still asleep at this hour," the raptor observed, "else you would recall that my diet does not include any of these squeaky little furry beasties. Let me remind you that nothing tickles my tastebuds faster than the native fish, the ones that have always been here. I mean the mountain whitefish, the arctic grayling, and especially the cutthroat trout. You should be aware, however, that I also dive for lake trout even when I'm not hungry. They are here only because someone, probably fishermen who were unaware of the threat to cutthroat, brought them here years ago and dumped them into Yellowstone Lake. They gorge on young cutthroat and have devoured much of the population."

39

"I actually heard a ranger once say," Nick remarked, "that the decline in numbers of cutthroat also endangers the survival of such trout predators as grizzlies, river otters, AND EVEN bald eagles. But didn't you tell me once that eagles enjoy a bird snack every so often?" the boy inquired.

"It's true, some do," Mike replied, "but I've never liked the flavor of grebes, or coots, while gulls and geese are too heavy to lug around. But I have to say one more time, I'm glad you're back. It was a long, dull winter here without you. I hope Geni returns from Jackson Hole soon," he added, echoing what Nick had just been thinking.

Turning their attention back to the rodent rendezvous, on the edge of the grove they caught sight of a coal black raven, perched on a stone some three feet high. It was squawking out instructions that sounded amazingly like the ones a caller provided at the Old Faithful Inn where, every so often, Nick, Geni, and their parents went to join the whoop and holler of an old-fashioned square dance. The more the raven screeched, the more Nick thought he understood what the bird was saying.

"Take your partner by the hand . . ."

"Do-si-do your corners . . ."

"Allemande left—allemande right . . ."

"Bow to your partner . . ."

At this point, the pieces fell neatly into place. The critters had formed three squares and were prancing around together obeying the raven's every command. "Just look at them go," Nick urged, "They are keeping time to the music, not only with their feet, but with other parts of their bodies."

"Hold on," Mike Mulligan interrupted, "not sure I get where the music comes in, unless it has something to do with that weird humming sound."

"The music is just as important as the rest of the action," Nick explained. "But I better start back at Old Faithful—it'll make what's going on here easier for you to follow."

Mr. Mulligan tilted his head to one side, his wordless way of persuading Nick to get on with the explanation.

"Well, at Old Faithful Inn it was like this. There were two musicians—one fiddled and the other played a saw. The music they made was perfect for a hoedown."

"Ho-who?" the raptor was still befuddled.

"It's a dance, usually involving eight in a group called a *square*. Sometimes it takes place in a barn so it's also known as a *barn dance*."

"Is that something barn owls do?" Mike wanted to know. "I run into them from time to time, even though unlike me they do their hunting at night. Can you imagine trying to spot a brown trout underwater in the dark?!" He shuddered at the thought.

Nick pointed out that here in the meadow there were no instruments, but instead a swarm of buzzing bees sounding just like a

41

musical saw. There was also a congregation of hummingbirds strumming fiddle-tunes as they whirred in and out of honeysuckle vines.

"Are you sure about all this?" Mike questioned doubtfully.

Watching all these critters stomp and twirl was more entertaining than watching people do the same thing, thought Nick. The pikas twitched their noses to the tempo of the music as they "dove for the oyster"; the rabbits kept the beat by flapping their ears as they "dug for the clam"; and the ground squirrels thumped their tails in perfect rhythm as they "do-si-doed" their partners. Nick could have stayed there all day, but realized that he would miss the hatch if he didn't hurry off to the river.

Chapter 8—Mike Mulligan *Enters* the Beaver Olympics

Together, the bird and the boy reached the water a little distance downstream from the best fishing spot and started to walk along the shore. At one point Soda Butte Creek widened and its current slowed, becoming more like a pond, because beavers had blocked it with a dam. As the pair approached, a second strange event was taking place—a whole colony of beavers, as many as 25 or 30, was playing some kind of game. Nick couldn't help himself. As much as he wanted to fish, he simply had to sit down on a log by the water's edge in order to satisfy his curiosity. Always snoopy, Mike flew overhead in low circles to get a better view.

At first, Nick thought the beavers were just hard at work building a lodge or repairing the dam in keeping with their "busy-beaver" reputation. But when he peered more closely, he realized they were divided into teams and were engaged in what appeared to be a relay race.

When one of the officials, an osprey, perched on a dead cottonwood branch, screeched its high-pitched "*Cree, Cree,*" the teams lined up quickly in assigned positions between two small aspen trees along the shore. Unfortunately, the game was interrupted by an unmistakable throbbing of wings when Mike Mulligan spotted the osprey, his eternal enemy. Diving at such great speed toward the osprey, the eagle could barely maneuver skillfully enough to avoid colliding with the cottonwood tree trunk. Amused by the eagle's near-miss, the osprey let out a cackle. The agitated eagle zoomed skyward to prepare for a second plunge toward the heckler.

But before Mike began his dive, Nick, eyes upward, hands on hips, shouted at his friend, "You have no idea how ridiculous you just looked—could the once-great attack raptor be so out of practice?"

Breathing hard, the eagle plopped onto Nick's shoulder. "Did you really think I looked comical?" he asked.

"No worse than an osprey screeching to organize a rodent sporting event."

"Well, okay, but those annoying fish-hawks can drive you up the wall—barn owls have much more class. Still, on the other hand, as you know, I just *hate* to look foolish."

When order had been restored, the beaver leader whacked his tail on the water with a resounding bang, clearly the starting signal. The first beaver on each team dove into the stream, swam to the other side, touched the bank with a paw, did a flip turn and sprinted, using his tail and webbed hind feet, as speedily as he could back to where he started. The instant he made contact, the second beaver dove in, then the third and the fourth, until each member of the team had raced across and back, encouraged by the hoots, squeals, and tail-thwacking applause of the beaver audience. Nick and Mike also noticed that there were two otters and a muskrat family among the spectators, clapping as enthusiastically as anyone.

"I wish I had my camera," Nick observed, "but I had no notion I'd run into anything as whacky-memorable as this. It should be called the *Beaver Olympics.*

Having fully regained his composure, Mike replied, "With my eagle eye, I have no need of a camera! Incidentally, you might be interested to know that the visiting team, called the *Loopies*, came all the way from Beaver Pond Loop near Mammoth Hot Springs; the locals, of course, are the Soda Butte *Beauties.*"

Although it was clear that there were to be more competitive events, the pair decided it was high time to be gone. Nick had already begun to see the early morning caddis hatch and knew if he didn't get a fly onto the water soon, it would be too late. He continued along the river's edge until he arrived at the fishing spot he considered his personal trout pool. The current moved slowly and the banks dropped off to form perfect hiding places for big cutthroat, the trout species abundant in the stream. He recalled telling Geni when they fished here a year ago that this beautiful native, the state fish of Wyoming, can be identified by the unique red-orange "cut" under its lower jaw.

"I know it really isn't my private fishing hole," he explained to Mike who was hovering overhead, "but I'm always a little miffed if I find another fisherman here."

Today he had the place all to himself. The young angler attached a fly, a *Chernobyl Ant*, to the tippet, the thinnest end of the fishing line. It is the section that attaches to the fly, so it must be lightweight, strong, and invisible to the fish.

He made a pretty good cast onto the stream and waited. No action. He tossed the fly out again . . . and again . . . and again. Nothing. In fact, over the next two hours, he must have changed flies a half dozen times—an *Orange Stimulator*, a *Royal Humpy*, and a *Dancing Green Drake*, to name a few—and cast fifty times or more as he waded up and down the stream. He couldn't understand why the fishing was so dull. In fact, compared to the critter square dance and the beaver Olympics, the fishing was so boring that Mike waved a lackluster "so long" as he soared away in search of better entertainment.

Just as Nick was beginning to think that lunch at home sounded a lot better than what he was accomplishing in the stream, he spotted the quick flash of the kind of movement in midstream that

45

could only be a trout. In an instant, he pulled the rod back over his shoulder, let out line, and tossed the fly out onto the water, a *Madame X*, one of the best to use in fast riffles. Much to his dismay, it landed with a loud splash.

For a moment, Nick was horrified to think that his sloppy cast had scared away the trout.

"I must be hyper to have flubbed the cast that badly," he muttered to himself. "Rats, now I've gone and *spooked* the fish."

Chapter 9—The Fisherman Meets the All-Elk Bugle Band

Hurriedly Nick made another cast, the best one yet. As he focused on the fly drifting closer and closer to where he had seen the flash, the surface of the water churned. In the next instant, an enormous hungry cutthroat rolled over and struck the *Madame* with force. Bracing himself on the streambottom, the young fisherman was ready, as the fish took the fly and sped with it into the current. Nick let the fish go pretty much where it wished, anywhere except under the bank, a place where Nick would be likely to lose his catch in a tangle of roots and sunken branches.

They fought each other for seven or eight minutes until the boy brought the cutthroat slowly into his net—without a doubt one of the bigger trout he'd ever caught and certainly large enough to feed a family. (Both Mom and Dad loved trout more than just about anything and knew how to make it dee-li-cious.) Instead of depositing the cutthroat in his creel, however, Nick moistened his hand to protect the fish, then held it up to admire. In a few seconds, he returned the prize gently to the water. A few years back, he had learned a technique called "Catch-and-Release," a practice fly fishermen respected. Nick's father had also taught him to flatten the barb on the hook to make it easy for the trout to slide off without injury.

Now that was pretty doggone exciting, he thought to himself, glowing with satisfaction.

Eager to report the fabulous fishing feat to his parents, he packed up his gear, and started home. Just as he reached the edge of the forest, he came upon yet another crazy scene, this one the strangest event in what he would certainly remember as *the weirdest day . . . ever.*

A small herd of elk had gathered in the meadow, but not, it seemed, to graze. Instead, they had formed a tuneful combo—more specifically an all-elk bugle band—and were playing their hearts out in concert. Never, in his frequent hikes through the park, had Nick seen or heard anything like this. Keeping a safe distance away, he stopped to take it all in. He quickly noticed that he was not the only member of the enthusiastic audience—six or seven grizzlies of varying ages, shapes, and sizes, all very well behaved. A pack of wolves, also good listeners, except for the pups who interrupted with occasional off-key howls; they had to be shushed by a growl and a snap from their mothers. Finally, the bison showed how desperately they wanted to join the ensemble by grunting in a most unmelodic way. They had to be restrained by the bandleader, a handsome bull elk with a pair of antlers so impressive that no one dared disobey him.

Finally, the bison settled down and the musicians began to play a medley of favorite pieces: *The Little Bugle Bull Medley*; *Fanfare for the Common Buck*; and *Fantasia for Horns and Hoofbeats*, to name a few. The applause after each composition was deafening. Even the bison, though disappointed not to participate, were so moved by the music that several large tears could be seen rolling down their shaggy cheeks.

For the third time that morning, Nick was blown away by what he had seen—first, a furry nibbler square dance; second, an eager beaver Olympics; and now a *gang* of bugling woodland musicians accompanied by a chorus of tone-deaf bison, plus an audience that included a cluster of appreciative carnivores. What in the world would he run into next?

The boy didn't have long to wonder. No sooner was he deep in the forest and about halfway home, when he had that eerie feeling that something was following him. As his premonition grew stronger, he'd take a step, stop, and look around hoping to discover whatever it was. At first, he didn't see anything, but each time he paused he was sure he heard a crunch behind him. The creature, trying to take one more stealthy step before coming to a halt, had crept a little closer.

Suddenly he spotted it, but instead of an "it" he detected a "them" standing up on hind legs. Noses in the air, they were peering out from behind a blue spruce, as if on the trail of something irresistible. There they were, two black bear cubs, not yet full grown, but definitely hefty enough to steer clear of.

Why are they snuffling me, Nick wondered, knowing that bears have highly skilled sniffers. Then, of course, he realized: *It has to be the remaining smell of trout still on my hands. If there's one thing that causes Blacky to drool even more than honey, it's the smell of fresh fish . . . these guys obviously want my cutthroat for a midday meal. OK. So at least we understand each other.*

The bears edged closer, looking innocently this way and that while making whistling noises to pretend that they had no interest in the boy or anything else nearby. But what concerned Nick the most was the safe bet that whenever one came upon a black juvenile furball, a full-grown female powerhouse was sure to be close at hand. Nick looked around to determine his options. He knew he couldn't outrun the bears—even cubs this age are quick on all fours. He strongly suspected that he couldn't out-talk them either, especially Mama Bear, assuming she would appear soon.

As Nick considered his choices, Mike Mulligan returned in time to notice the drama involving his friend and the approaching bear twins, who seemed to grow larger with every step. As if on cue, Brunetta appeared, stomping along a few feet behind.

Chapter 10—Time for a Magic Berry

"Quick, old buddy, time for a magic berry, if you have them," the raptor called out, realizing that the two of them were no match for Mama and her pair of chubby cubbies.

Nick reached into his pack, pulled out the branch of berries, and gobbled one down. In seconds, he began to transform. Tall for a 14-year-old, he was aware that, as all four of his new paws hit the ground, he shrank to about two feet in length. His skin changed into sable-colored fur; and a tail with five or six black rings sprouted where tails are always located. His most distinctive feature, however, was the mask of dark fur around his eyes. It is thought that this coloring helps the raccoon—for that's what Nick had become—with night vision, supporting the animal's, as well as the barn owl's, favorite time to hunt.

Adjusting to his new identity, Nick recalled his dad mentioning that after a raccoon snatched a fish from the stream—its favorite food—it was often seen appearing to rinse the fish off in the water. "That explains," Dad had continued, "why early Native Americans gave it the name 'ahrah-koon-em' meaning one who rubs, scrubs and scratches."

"Just remember, old buddy, as a raccoon, you have the brainpower to outsmart this bruin trio," Mike Mulligan emphasized, "or at least the shrewdness to appeal to Mama's maternal instincts."

Although raccoons are canny and clever, they are no match for a mother black bear—as Mike fully understood—when she is protecting her young. Turning his attention to the cubs, Nick was aware that one smallish but scrappy raccoon would come out on the short end in a brawl with two cubs already big enough to consider themselves pretty rough-and-tough dudes. However, with its claws and almost human-like hands, a raccoon is an excellent climber. Nick realized that the way to avoid a scuffle was to put some altitude between himself and the bear threesome. His plan, which he speedily put into action, was to escape by clambering up the tall cottonwood only a few feet away. The trout smell might cause the cubs to climb up after him, but he felt confident that if Mama preferred to keep an eye on the action from below, he could deal with her cubbies.

His prediction about Mama Bear was soon confirmed—she was one of the non-climbers. She sauntered over, stood below, and looked up toward the raccoon-boy sitting on a branch, feeling safely out of reach . . . at least from her.

"Just exactly what is that *dee-li-cious* aroma that seems to be clinging to your raccoon coat?" mama bear inquired.

"I suppose it's a cutthroat trout smell," answered the recent fisherman. "It must be leftover from the one I caught this morning."

"Mm . . . and pray tell . . . whatever became of that . . . uh . . . cutthroat trout?" she asked.

"Put it back in Soda Butte Creek," was his reply.

"Well fancy that. Put it back did you? said Mama. "Why you must be the most ignorant raccoon I've ever bumped into. First, you give away my family's number-one favorite *ree-past*, and second, you make *your-own-self* available as a dinner substitute by scooting up that tree. Don't you know anything? Bear young-fry love to climb trees, especially when there's a reward up there waiting for them."

51

No sooner had she spelled out the danger he was in than Nick felt a jiggling of the limb beneath him. He tried to crawl away, but for some strange reason he couldn't budge. Peering down, he saw the reason why—one of the cubs had clamped a paw on top of his tail-stripes. There was young *Blacky* grinning hungrily up at him, beginning to lick the raccoon's *right* paw. While the inexperienced ring-tailed boy puzzled over how to get out of this mess, another figure entered the treetop scene. Cub number two eased onto the limb, tweaked Nick's whiskers, and started to lick his *left* paw.

Keeping a keen eye on the goings-on, Mama Bear called up toward the threesome huddled on a single cottonwood branch. "Now you've done it. Like I told you, those young fellas will shoot up a tree for the pure fun of it. But the fish smell on your paws is an appetite turn-on. At this point, nothing will satisfy them till their bellies are full."

"Any chance we could talk it over up here?" Nick wondered.

"Oh my, there you go again showing your ignorance. These two are much too young for conversation—in fact, they've only been growling for a couple of weeks. Before that you should have heard these puppies squeal! But tell you what, I'm going to let them know first, it's time to *dee-scend*, and second, that any bear cub wolfing down anything as peculiar as you for supper is likely to suffer serious *diss-peps-sia*, if you know what I mean."

Mama Bear turned her attention to the cubs. "You two young'uns get on down here and we'll hunt up an anthill, a honeycomb, or maybe a patch of blueberry bushes."

Somewhat reluctantly, but already drooling over visions of honeycomb, the cubs started down. As the raccoon watched the rambunctious twins descend, he failed to see the bald eagle that landed on the branch just above his tufted ears.

"Now I could surely grow to like that mama," Mike Mulligan declared, startling the raccoon-boy whose attention had been elsewhere. "She not only succeeded in convincing her cubs there's a better meal available than a *peculiar raccoon*, but she saved me from the risky business of having to swoop down to rescue my pal from the jaws of those two hungry fur-balls. We'll never know if I could actually get airborne with such a cute, but chubby critter as you in my talons."

As the setting sun sent brilliant shades of red and green across Bison Peak and Mount Hornaday, Nick, again a suntanned 14-year-old started to gather his things for the hike home. He stopped what he was doing long enough for Mike Mulligan, curious about the delay, to land gently on his shoulder.

"Something on your mind, old buddy?"

Well, speaking of *peculiar*," Nick began, "sitting up there on the limb with those two ravenous bear boys put an odd thought in my head. What if a magic berry turned me into, let's say, a *mottled sculpin*, or a *redside shiner*? Aren't they all high on your list of suppertime favorites?" he added, showing off his knowledge of native fish.

The eagle quietly gave him a peck on the cheek, then stated firmly, "Very nitpicking of you to pick two fish that no one has ever heard of. Once again, your memory has betrayed you. It appears you have forgotten that a year ago, when you were a rainbow trout for a day, I hauled you in my claws, not once but twice, puffing and panting for breath, to and from Secret Valley Creek."

"Good answer, Señor Mike, even though you surely knew I was only pulling your talon. But as a peace offering, c'mon home with me—I'm sure Mom can dig up an uncooked scrap of that rainbow left over from last night's dinner."

Smiling happily, Mike Mulligan nodded his approval.

Yellowstone Park's #1 Detective Agency

Chapter 11—Trouble in the General Stores

Nick was surprised at breakfast when Dad announced that there had been a break-in during the night at the general store in Canyon Village, not far from their cabin.

"Moreover," he added, "whoever did it made a real mess of the place, smashing bottles and jars, dumping stuff off the shelves, and leaving vegetables, fruit, and loaves of bread in bits and pieces up and down the aisles. How would you feel about dropping by to help clean up?"

The news came as quite a shocker. But bad as the incident was, it would get even worse a few days later when the same thing occurred several miles away at the general store in Lake Village.

"Sure, I'll go," Nick said, in answer to the question, "and I bet Geni will come help, too."

"Give her a call," Mom suggested, while I put on some old clean-up clothes and make us a snack."

Mom knew better than most that anticipation of a snack could persuade ravenous fourteen year-olds to do almost anything.

They met Geni near the cabin she and her family rented, and soon the foursome was filling garbage bags with all manner of trash that littered the floor in the Canyon Village store. After dealing with the larger items—plastic bottles, boxes, vegetables and fruit all smashed and soggy—the assistant manager brought out brooms and mops to sweep up the little bits and swab down the sticky spots.

When finished, they sat outside at one of the picnic tables to munch Mom's snack of apples and nuts, to which the assistant added his thanks in the form of double scoop ice cream cones. Nick polished off strawberry-vanilla swirl and Geni, more creative, slurped on chocolate-pistachio fudge twist.

On the way home, they couldn't talk about anything other than the break-in—how much stuff had been wasted, how many hours it had taken to clean up, and who could possibly be responsible for all the damage. Before reaching the cabins it was clear, without actually saying so, that they were fired up, like a pair of detectives, to investigate this occurrence and, if possible, discover who the culprits were.

The morning after the next break-in at Lake Village, the teens walked down to a favorite place in search of inspiration. That it happened to be called "Inspiration Point" made them hopeful they would come up with a good idea or two. Along the road they passed the enormous granite boulder, a landmark bigger than a barn, that had been part of the Beartooth Mountain Range miles away before a glacier moved it to the spot some 80,000 years ago. Both paused to press their hands against the stone for luck, then continued through the forest to the observation point high above the Grand Canyon of the Yellowstone River. Whenever Nick saw the views of Upper and Lower Falls, he felt a lump in his throat because it was so spectacular.

"*¡Qué magnifico!*" exclaimed Geni.

"*¡Si, es impresionante!*" Nick boomed out, pleased that his few minutes in the Spanish dictionary last evening gave him an edge.

"*¡Un hombre tan bueno!* What a guy!" she said, "by the end of the summer you will certainly be ready for Spanish III!"

56

Nick couldn't tell if she was serious or teasing. In either case, he silently vowed to get back to the dictionary again. Now they sat on the picnic table bench at Inspiration Point, determined to figure out who was up to no good at the general stores.

"Do you think there's anything we can do?" Geni wondered.

"I really don't know," he answered, after hearing the details from his dad. "Whoever it is must be the same person to have done exactly the same thing in two different places."

"It sure was a mess, wasn't it," she noted. "It was almost as if someone had carefully made up a work order listing items to smash in order to repeat so precisely in both stores. Bottles of soda, honey-flavored cereal, large jars of jam and jelly, lots of fruit including big melons, and a variety of veggies, mostly fat round things like *calabazas y berenjena*s"

"Pumpkins and eggplant," Nick translated, even managing to surprise himself. "But nothing made as big a mess as the watermelons. I like your list—it makes me wonder why most everything opened or in shreds was also sugary."

At that very moment, in a noisy flutter of feathers, Mike Mulligan crash-landed on the picnic table, almost causing the teenagers to flop over backward in surprise.

"Some landing, Champ! The raptor Olympics is definitely out for you!" Nick exclaimed, not wanting to admit how glad he always was when his eagle friend came looking for them. "Can't you see we are having an important conversation? If you want to help us, do you know anything about what has happened at the two general stores?"

Scrutinizing them down the length of his yellow beak, the eagle responded, "Luckily I have arrived in the *nick* of time (no personal reference intended, old buddy). Together, with the benefit of legendary eagle-judgment, we can definitely solve this mystery."

As usual Mike stared out of those penetrating yellow eyes as if, understanding most things better than anyone, he could barely tolerate the opinions of two fourteen-year-olds whose views, like it or not, he was forced to put up with. After sitting there for another twenty minutes trying to come up with a plan, the teens wandered off toward home, with Mike in the air yelling down to them, "Straight as the eagle flies." Careening back in their direction every minute or so, he made sure the twosome was following their airborne guide.

The next day, the novice detectives made no new progress. As for the creation of a plan to catch the guilty party, by the end of the week their interest in the topic had generally begun to evaporate. Then suddenly, once again in the middle of breakfast, the phone rang. Dad returned to the table to announce, "There's been another break-in, this time at Grant Village. The result is the same—a total trashing of the general store."

For the second time, the foursome agreed to help, jumped into the truck, and rode south past Lake Village to join the clean-up crew at Grant. it was easy to see that the same assortment of items lay all about, torn, shattered, and strewn . . . AND, as before, a sweet odor permeated the building.

Chapter 12—Mike Mulligan Joins the Investigation

Hoping more impatiently than ever for a brainstorm, Nick and Geni returned to Inspiration Point to review what they knew. There they found Mike Mulligan strutting back and forth on the picnic table. "Learn anything new, by chance?" the eagle wanted to know.

"*Esto es muy difícil*, these strange events" Geni replied. "We have examined everything thoroughly, but only the similarities provide any helpful clues."

"With you so far," said the eagle, "but consider this for a minute. Can you remember if anyone has mentioned how the vandals got in?"

"I think the assistant manager at Canyon admitted they couldn't figure it out," Geni recalled. "No door or window was broken and everything was locked up as usual."

"Let's walk over there and try to get the answer to Mike's question, "Nick suggested, "talk to whoever's in charge today, and have another look around."

Mike Mulligan urged, "Let's go!" as he bobbed his white head up and down in approval. When they arrived at Canyon, they spotted the manager, Mr. Schwarzwald, busy helping customers. Waiting until he was free, they poked around for clues on their own, with Mike perched on Nick's shoulder.

"Schwarzwald is a good German name," Geni whispered. "It means *Black Forest*, a famous mountain area near Baden-Baden where tourists go. Many of Europe's great rivers begin there, including the *Blue Danube*."

59

"Yeah. And did you know," Nick threw in, "the Black Forest is where Hansel and Gretel stumbled onto the witch?"

"I'll take Yellowstone," Mike retorted.

Though somewhat puzzled by the presence of the eagle, manager Schwarzwald came smiling toward the threesome. "Ah, my friends, you young people and your eagle are special. I have heard that you helped clean up at Grant Village as you did here—that was such a nice thing. Now what can I do for you?"

"Can you tell us, Mr. Schwarzwald," Nick asked, "if anyone has any notion how the intruders got in?"

"Sorry to say, it remains an *enigma*," he answered, wrinkling his forehead in frustration. "We have looked everywhere, inside and out, and have not found any possible explanation."

"It is interesting," Geni murmured, leaning toward Nick, "*enigma* is the same word in Spanish

"I'm glad to know," he whispered back. "I bet it pops up in Spanish III." And then to the manager again, "It's all a very curious business, isn't it? Do you mind if we have a look around?"

After getting the manager's okay, they spent a few minutes inside but spotted nothing more unusual than what they had already seen while cleaning the two stores. But never having thought to investigate outside in their previous search, they began looking carefully at everything within ten feet of the building's outer walls.

"*¡Nada!* Absolutely nothing!" Geni grumbled after they had covered every inch without success. "I just don't get it."

"Why don't we go around one more time," Mike Mulligan proposed, "this time very slowly. Nick, you look to the left, Geni to the right, and I'll be sure to check it out up high, above eye level."

Soon after the search began, Mike Mulligan flew from Nick's shoulder, circled low over the roof, planning to inspect the skylight and the area around it. As they approached a corner that was partially hidden by a grove of aspen trees, the eagle spotted freshly broken branches and scratch marks on the trunk of a tree near the roof.

"Well I'll be a Red-Naped Sapsucker!" the eagle exclaimed. "I wish you could see this. There are muddy prints everywhere," he reported, his eyes sparkling over the significance of the discovery. "And the skylight glass is smudged as if someone rolled on it after wallowing in one of Yellowstone's famous mudpots, perhaps *Black Dragon Caldron.*"

"*¡Estupendo!*" Geni exclaimed.

"Tee-rific!" Nick repeated, in his native tongue . . . *almost.*

After absorbing the details, Nick and Geni hustled back inside and peered up at the ceiling skylight, an opening three or four feet square. A new and meaningful clue had fallen into place.

"Mr. Schwarzwald," Nick called, "is that skylight tightly fixed or does it open easily when you push or pull it?"

"Whenever it gets stuffy, we lift the skylight with that long pole over against the wall to bring in some fresh air, and we rarely remember to fasten it afterwards. Why do you ask?"

"No reason," the boy replied. "Just curious."

Staring at each other, the threesome simultaneously realized that they had two clues: first, the similarity of the various kinds of foodstuffs littering the floor; and now, confirmed by the detective *with the eagle eyes*, visible signs that the intruders had slipped in through the skylight. In order to test this theory, they decided to ask Nick's dad to take them over to Lake Village. Perhaps they could spot something the second time that they had missed the first. Once again, Mike Mulligan led them home where Dad agreed to be *chauffeur* the next day, though Nick detected a mild lack of enthusiasm for the task.

Despite Dad's preference for reading the newspaper over a second cup of coffee, he agreed to be the chauffeur. Geni declared that she was raring to go. "For sure we will learn something *importante y nuevo*. But also I love that your father used *chauffeur*, a good French word."

It was a struggle for Nick not to inform her that *chauffeur* was also "a good English word," but he didn't want to sound like his feathery know-it-all buddy.

Chapter 13—The #1 Detectives Assess the Clues

The next morning, just as it was time to leave for Grant Village, there was more bad news—a fourth ransacking, this one in the store at Old Faithful. As they suspected, it was just like the previous three.

"The mystery becomes more intriguing with each new break-in," Geni said, when Nick called to let her know. "Let's just hustle over there, if it's OK with your Papa. It's close enough and the clues will be fresher."

"Fine with me," Dad agreed to the plan. "Tell Geni we'll be there in a few."

While Dad was getting ready, Mike Mulligan swooped in just long enough to let them know, "Head off without me for a bit. I'll catch up with you later."

"Can't imagine that the eagle's message doesn't have something to do with missing breakfast because he overslept," Geni observed in the car. "As usual, the appetite comes first."

(Having long since learned the vital lesson of knowing when to hold his tongue, Nick knew better than to mention Geni's own appetite issues.)

They packed up and headed to Old Faithful where, as usual, crowds of tourists were busily snapping away at the geysers with their iPhones. There are almost two hundred geysers near Old Faithful Village, one or more erupting every few minutes.

As they entered the general store, Geni pointed, "Look, there is a skylight in the corner, and much of the clutter is on the floor directly underneath . . . including the bakery shelves all turned over."

Let's have a look outside," Nick answered, "and I bet I know what we'll find."

Sure enough, in less than five minutes they detected visible scrapes high up the trunk and newly splintered branches on a tree near the skylight.

"Wonder where *you-know-who* has zoomed off to?" Geni reflected. "He could easily check the roof for evidence, if he were here."

"I'm surprised he hasn't returned," Nick replied, "since one of his pleasures in life is to point out where we've gone wrong."

They left Old Faithful and were dropped off close to the Inspiration Point trail where they hoped to find Señor Mulligan. Sure enough, who should be perched atop the granite boulder? None other than the missing *ravenous raptor*. Once again, he flew down and pranced on the picnic table, his predictable lead-in before communicating something of great consequence, perhaps in this case the details of his breakfast. What they didn't know as they waited patiently for him to get on with it, was that they were in for a rather embarrassing surprise.

"While you were detecting here at Old Faithful, I zoomed down to Grant Village. It seemed worthwhile, not having looked the scene over before, to discover whether there was anything new to be learned from the break-in there."

Nick looked at Geni; Geni looked at Nick. Both teens suddenly had red faces.

"Yeah, I know," the eagle went on, "you believed I had overslept, missed breakfast, and was out preparing *Trout Florentine* at river's edge. In fact, I may have turned up a new clue. When we looked around at the Canyon Village store the second time, I noticed a broken clock lying in the mess on the floor. It read 4 a.m. When I was checking things out at Grant Village, I dug another clock out of the trash pile and guess what—it had also stopped at almost the same time. So what do you think the clocks tell us?"

"I'd say there's a good chance that the break-ins occurred around 4 a.m., give or take five or ten," Nick concluded, adding, for the benefit of a beaming Detective Mulligan, "Thanks to you, one more good clue!"

After several minutes, Geni turned and spoke thoughtfully. "The more I think about it, the more I want to tell you about an idea that came to me on the way back from Old Faithful."

"Great! Tell us," Nick urged, "and then I've got an idea to mention that just popped into my head."

"I'm all ears," croaked Mike Mulligan, whose hearing was keen, despite not having visibly protruding ears like his human buddies.

"*¡Muy bien!* Listen to this. There are six general stores in the park and four have been *hit by*. . . what's the word for *banditos*? The incidents took place in an order that we should consider—Canyon, Lake, Grant, and Old Faithful. When you study the list of villages carefully, does it tell you anything?"

"Let me guess. No, that would take too long. What have you come up with that might help us?" Nick was eager to know.

"Beginning at Canyon, the general stores have been struck clockwise in geographic order, not only the first four, but it could include all six if you list them that way," she continued. 'In fact, the locations form a circle that encloses the center of the park, an area surrounded by the main road. And, if you move in that circle it's a pretty short distance from one store to the next."

"Mmm, quite interesting," Nick agreed, "but what exactly does it mean?"

"Begin with the fact that there are two general stores that haven't been hit, Mammoth and Roosevelt. Could the order so far be a signal to us that Mammoth Hot Springs, the next one in the loop, might be the upcoming target?"

"Cool," he flashed her a quick look. "And it so happens that it may be worthwhile to combine my idea with yours and Mike's. Listen to this and see what you think. There were five days between the Canyon vandalism and the one at Lake Village; it was four days after Lake that Grant was struck; and then three days from Grant to the break-in at Old Faithful. If it's possible that these clues are putting us on the right track, the next place, like you suggest, will be Mammoth Hot Springs. Plus, if the other clues make sense, it should happen in *two days*, meaning the day after tomorrow, around 4 a.m.

"*¡Yo lo creo!* I believe it!" Geni stated, full of excitement. "So what do we do to get ready?"

Now it was Mike's turn. Having continued pacing back and forth on the table, he stopped abruptly right in front of the teenagers, ruffled his tail-feathers to get their full attention, and spoke directly to Nick.

"Good buddy, don't you think the moment has come to share our *other secret* with Geni?"

That did it! thought Nick, his heart pounding, his mind working overtime in anticipation. Ever since he and Geni became friends, the boy had been wondering when it would be the right time, the perfect moment, to share *the secret of the magic berries*. Even more complicated, when, if ever, would they gulp them down together? Because of the four break-ins and the clear message from Mike, it appeared to be now!

Chapter 14—Geni Learns the Second Astonishing Secret

It had been almost a year since Geni had learned the first secret—that Nick and Mike Mulligan could talk to each other in English—as could she, having been welcomed into *su fraternidad*, their special group. ("I live in Yellowstone Park, USA," the raptor had said. "What language would you have me speak?") Now, at last, Nick shared with her the story of saving the young eagle from a coyote attack, then nursing him back to health. How Mike Mulligan had given him a branch with magic berries, and how when Nick swallowed them over the following weeks he had morphed into an eagle, a trout, a wolf pup, and a mountain goat. Also, how, as a porcupine, he had rescued Mike a second time by driving quills into a malicious eagle hunter about to pull the trigger of his rifle. And finally, how the grateful raptor returned with a new batch of magic berries just as his friend was about to run out.

"Then there was that scary moose-painting moment," Nick recalled, "when you nearly were the victim of a mountain lion. Along came a grizzly bear that chased the big cat up the side of the cliff while an eagle was soaring overhead keeping an eye on the action. I'm sure you remember all that?"

"How could I possibly forget?" she shuddered. "And I may still have bruises where the bear knocked me down. It makes me shiver just to remember how awful it was—*¡estaba muy aterrador!*—I was terrified!"

A moment later, deep in thought, the girl hesitated. Then her expression changed as she stared straight at the other two and spoke softly. "It was Mike who went to warn you that I was in trouble, wasn't it? And because of the berry, you turned into the big hairy hulk that pushed me out of the way and whacked the wild cat up over the cliff."

"Right so far, Geni," their raptor friend agreed.

Nick remained still while she struggled to accept what she had begun to fully understand. Then the eagle broke the silence. "If you are ready, Geni, and if you trust us, then it is time to discover the magic of the berries for yourself."

"Don't you remember, you two bobos, that a year ago I made it *absolutamente claro* that I want to be *loco* with you?"

"*¡Superestupendísimo!*" Mike declared, enjoying his recently adopted Spanish exclamation.

Nick felt a similar excitement, though he quietly kept his feelings to himself.

When they met the following day, without uttering a word, they knew that the time had come to plan the next move, the move they hoped would enable them to learn who had been making a mess of the general stores. By the end of the afternoon they had decided, with a fair amount of confidence, what they were going to do.

Several hours later, at midnight, the teens met again at the granite boulder. No sooner had they arrived than they became aware of a whirring noise above. There in a beam of moonlight was a dapper fellow sporting a yellow beak, white head and tail-feathers. The pair quickly admitted that, as always, it was a good thing to have Mike along.

Now that they were ready for action, Nick lifted the mysterious branch out of his backpack, plucked two berries for the teens to gulp down together. Slowly but steadily, the changes began to take shape. As it was her first-ever magic berry experience, Geni's reaction was total astonishment. Sensing the changes, she touched her new gray-brown coat, tufted ears, black-tipped tail, and of all things, a gorgeous display of whiskers. Accustomed to morphing into wild creatures, Nick waited calmly as dense dark fur, white hair on his throat and chest, a silvery face and thick, full tail replaced the body of this 14-year-old boy.

When the transformations were complete, each exclaimed in turn, "Omigosh, you are a perfect bobcat!" and, "*¡Increíble!* You are the fiercest looking skunk I have ever seen!"

"Skunk!" the boy grumbled, his dignity offended. "Black and white coloring, short legs and bushy brown tail don't necessarily add up to *skunk*."

But in the next moment, ignoring her error in identification, he started to feel quite full of himself. He had become, pound for pound, the most ferocious animal in the park, *a wolverine*. No other creature, even the mighty griz, would tangle with one if it could be avoided. Also called a *nasty cat*, the wolverine is the largest member of the weasel family.

After huffily spelling out the differences between skunks and wolverines, Nick headed off with his friends toward Mammoth Hot Springs, feeling certain that the trespassers would show themselves.

As the twosome loped along through the darkness, guided from above by a raptor with 20-20 night vision, Nick shared with

70

Geni his knowledge of the pre-dawn sky. Singling out several easy-to-spot constellations, he briefly told her the stories of three of the best.

"There is Perseus who killed the monster, Medusa, while flying on Pegasus, the famous winged horse. Next, the constellation of Orion, the great hunter, not only because of the well-known versions of the myth, but because it includes two of the brightest stars in the sky, *Rigel* and *Betelgeuse*. You can't see *Centaurus* because it is in the Southern Sky, but I know you'd like the story of Chiron, half man, half horse, the wisest and most just of all the Centaurs.

"*Las estrellas son hermosas.* The stars are so beautiful. Perhaps you could help me learn more about them and I could help you with Spanish?"

Her suggestion put Nick on cloud nine! Once he had thought of offering her fishing lessons in exchange for help in Spanish. But he had delayed, edgy that she'd be ticked by the implication that he considered himself a better fisherman. Her offer made everything simpler.

But it wasn't simpler for long. "It so happens that I spend most of my time closer to the stars and planets than either of you earthlings," announced a certain raptor with a hint of irritation, "but to tell the truth, my Spanish can stand a bit of *augmentation,* too."

"*Aug-what??*" the bobcat inquired. "Seems likely related to the Spanish *aumento.*"

"Right on, Geni, Both words refer to something getting larger, but best to ignore him when he gets like this," the wolverine advised.

71

The eagle put on view his best *you-have-offended-me* look before soaring off into the dark sky. "I'll meet you at Mammoth Village in a twinkling—star that is—but till then I have important business to attend to," and was gone.

Chapter 15—Three Sherlocks Solve the Case

Bounding steadily through the woods, it didn't take long to get to Mammoth Hot Springs where, just before 4 a.m., Nick and Geni put their plan into action. The bobcat climbed a tree next to the general store, lifted the skylight, right where they thought it would be, and sprang down inside. Making her way to the delivery door, she was able to turn the lock with her teeth to let the wolverine in. Then they looked for a strategic hiding place.

In less than ten minutes, they heard scratching sounds on the roof, causing them to stare up breathlessly as the ceiling window was lifted. Through the skylight and down into the store came not one, not two, but three intruders. First came a mother black bear, who had to use super-Bruno effort to squeeze through the barely bear-sized opening; she was followed by two half-grown cubs. Nick wondered if it might have been the same trio that had chased the raccoon-boy up a tree only a few days earlier.

No sooner had the three bears leapt down into the store than the mother knocked over the bakery shelf and began to tear open and devour packaged cakes and loaves of bread. The first cub ripped the plastic covers off the produce bins, splattering several melons on the floor. Then he started slurping up the syrupy pulp. While all this was going on, the other cub was tearing into containers of lemonade, cranberry juice, and chocolate milk. It was finally clear why the vandals focused on sweetness—to them it was *bear nectar* and *ambrosia*.

Signaling each other silently, Geni and Nick agreed that it was time to go into action. They dashed out of the dark corner where they were hiding, crashing into the cubs at such velocity that both fuzzballs tumbled over and over and finally sat up looking bewildered. The mother was another story altogether. The bobcat crept cautiously toward her, while the wolverine snuck down a different aisle and waited, watching and listening, ready for whatever might occur.

Seconds later, the bobcat sped around the corner, the mama bear roaring at her heels. But just as Blacky was about to catch up with Geni-Bob, Wolver-Nick rushed toward the bear, uttering a fierce snarl that only wolverines, spitting mad, can make.

Mama Bear, speechless for an instant, quickly regained her composure. "Just what d'you two think yer doin'?" she growled. "How'd you get in here anyway, and why are you pesterin' us?"

"We are the Number 1 Detective Agency in Yellowstone, protecting the park from critters like you," Nick snapped. Nick's voice caused the bear to pull up in surprise, as if the way he spoke produced a flicker of recognition.

"You ree-mind me of an odd raccoon I ran into last week—but, of course, that's ree-diculous."

Her puzzlement gave the teen-agers a sought-after opportunity. Leaping the few feet that separated them, the wolverine sank his fangs into the bear's hind leg. Emitting a howl of pain, she wheeled around and, as she spun, the big kitty, back on the attack, chomped on the other leg. As the she-bear shifted her focus to the

73

bobcat, the wolverine flew at her again and for an instant clung to her back snapping at her ears while the wild cat wound up with the bear's stubby tail clenched between her teeth.

This double assault proved to be almost too much for the she-bear. But then the two cubs, overcoming their brief confusion, dashed over to back up their mother. Re-energized, Mama-Bear reared up on her hind legs looking larger than ever.

Staring her attackers down, she rumbled, "Don't you dare touch my babies or I promise there will be bar-bee-cued bobcat for supper!"

At this point, the two detectives and the three bears, realizing the time had come for one and all to head for the hills, burst through the back door and split into opposite directions as the first rays of dawn lit up the eastern sky. The local elk population, munching and chilling out on the village greenery, paused to stare at the odd scene in which three black bears were tearing off in a northerly direction while a bobcat and a wolverine hustled away toward the South. Even at this early hour, several humans, edging too close to the protective elk mothers and calves trying to snap a prize-winning photo, were dumbfounded by the bewildering spectacle.

Stopping to look back, the bobcat and the wolverine witnessed quite an interesting drama taking place outside the store. Just as the three bears were beating a frantic retreat past the colorful limestone terraces, there came a young bald eagle—guess who?—and right behind him three park rangers, each appearing to carry some kind of weapon. *Ping, Ping, Ping* went the tranquilizer dart-guns, and moments later the bears, perfectly okay, were lying limp on the ground.

Nick and Geni glanced at each other for the umpteenth time in the past few hours and wordlessly agreed that it was time to head for home. It was only a matter of minutes before they were struck by the radiant colors of daybreak settling on the granite boulder where Mike was waiting.

"There you are, and not a moment too soon," he chirped. "I was beginning to think about organizing a search party."

Soon the two teens were their old non-furry selves, safe and sound, but a little *fatigados*, Geni commented, from the exertion of the early morning detective activity. After the three friends revisited with the eagle the *bear details* of the adventure, Nick looked over at Geni as they were leaving for their cabins and teased, "As good-looking a bobcat as you were, I'm glad your whiskers are gone."

"And I'm glad," Geni observed, "that one of my detective partners was a wolverine instead of a skunk."

When the three sleuths met at Inspiration Point the next day, Nick was more than a little excited to report the latest news, hot off the press. "Dad heard from the rangers this morning that the vandals had been caught in the act, thanks, it was reported, to the very peculiar behavior of a bald eagle."

(Mike cocked his head innocently to one side.)

"Apparently the bird woke everyone in the ranger station by dropping pebbles on the metal roof. Then," the boy went on, "by flapping his wings vigorously, he led three of the rangers over to the store. There they spotted and tranquilized a black bear sow and two cubs who had just wrecked the place. Almost certainly, the rangers

75

concluded, these were the same bears that broke into the other four locations."

"By now," Nick concluded his report, "the critters have been hauled away and turned loose in the back country, many miles from any general store."

"*¡Muy Bueno!*" Geni observed with a smile. "I am glad the bears are OK—I am also relieved that they won't be back to do damage in the villages again soon. But there are two things I still don't understand. How in the world were bears able to decide the order of the stores to break into? And what made them choose to raid each new place following a number pattern starting with a gap of five days, then four, three, and finally two?"

Nick pondered these questions, before suggesting, "Let's start with a possible answer to both questions. Having learned where they could gorge themselves so easily, the ability to control their appetites became shorter and shorter, affecting both time and distance. And possibly the other answer is that by carefully leaving clues near each other in a circle they were testing the shrewdness of the *#1 best detectives in Yellowstone Park.*"

"Good thinking, old buddy," the raptor agreed. "Won't black bears ever learn that they're no match for the super-intelligent!"

"The *who?*" Geni grinned broadly.

"But wait," Nick continued, barely containing a burst of laughter, "I forgot to tell you something important. The ranger revealed one more tidbit to Dad, and are you going to love this! Aside from the curious eagle performance, the rangers were also baffled to find tufts of bobcat and wolverine fur on the floor of the market.

So the friends gave each other a high five, said *adios y hasta luego* and set out for well-deserved *siestas* at home.

A Fish, the Bear & Me

Chapter 16—Lessons on Fishing the Madison

On a sunny day, quite early in the morning, Nick left the family's cabin, fishing rod in hand, and trekked off through the trees. Although he and Geni usually fished together, he was alone this morning. Geni had decided instead to take the landscape watercolor class the park was offering.

"It won't be long before museums will be hounding you for paintings to hang on their walls," Nick had kidded the previous day.

"You are so kind," she replied, adding that, "you are also the *maestro de exageración*, the master of exaggeration."

The trail led him through a lovely wood filled with wildflowers—bright yellow Rocky Mountain cinquefoil, and elegant blue and white Colorado columbine—and buzzing with the sound of insects and birds. He spotted a multicolored pigeon-like bird, its grayness tinged with blue, brown, and pink. Recently, with help from one of the rangers, he identified it as a Eurasian Collared Dove, a newcomer to the U.S. named after the black half-collar on its neck.

The boy thought it interesting that its name, originating in ancient Greek mythology, refers to the tale of a servant who bitterly laments being underpaid. The gods change her into a dove whose call—coo, coo, coo—mourns her low salary forever. The ranger also told him that the dove had quickly become a favorite raptor food. The recollection caused him to wonder what his eagle buddy was up to.

He saw three mule deer, a porcupine, and numerous ground squirrels as he continued along the way. He also passed an active

78

beehive, stopping to admire the large honeycomb dripping with honey.

After about thirty minutes, Nick came to the edge of the Madison River, not only one of the most beautiful streams in Yellowstone, but also, as he was well aware, one of the great fly-fishing waters of the West.

He pulled a fly box out of the pocket of his fishing vest and selected a Royal Wulff, a red-and-white fly that was easy to see as it floated on the water's surface. The Royal Wulff was one of Nick's favorites, especially because it was named after Lee Wulff, renowned fly fisherman and conservationist.

Carefully attaching the fly to the tippet, Nick made a few practice casts, partly to limber up his arm, but also to run some line off the reel. When he was ready, he whipped the line back over his right shoulder, paused, then snapped the rod smartly forward causing the line to pass over his head. At the end of the cast, the fly landed gently on the water—important because a splash could spook the fish. To attract the fish, the fly needed to appear just like the tasty insect it imitated, in this case a mayfly, one of a group of ancient aquatic insects that also includes the dragonfly. The Royal Wulff slipped into the current and started slowly downstream, wiggling a little, as if trying to swim.

Knowing he had made a good cast, with eyes focused on the fly, Nick waited expectantly for the trout to rise to the surface and slurp up its best meal of the day.

Nothing happened. Slowly the young fisherman reeled in the line and cast again to a slightly different place. Again, a good cast, and again . . . no bite.

For the next two hours, Nick walked along the river, repeatedly sending dry flies out onto perfect trout locations, riffles where rainbow trout waited for insects to come drifting by, or pools along the banks where brown trout rested, alert for the next floating morsel.

No luck. He changed to a Golden Stonefly Stinger; next he tried a salmon fly called a *Sofapillow*, the largest aquatic insect in the U.S.; then to a Rio Grande King; and finally an olive Wooly Bugger, a streamer fly that sinks a few inches beneath the surface. But always the same result—no bites. He was not happy.

Before he left the cabin, Nick's mother had given him a hug and declared, "Well, my clever fisherboy, since the rangers have allowed you and Dad each to keep a fish, if you catch a big one, we'll have it for supper tonight. You know how your father loves to grill rainbow fresh from the stream, especially if he can get you to clean it.

Big one? he reflected, rather discouraged, *when I haven't even scared up a minnow.*

As Nick weighed what to do now, Mike Mulligan swooped down next to him. "What's up, Buddy Boy? You look a little glum. Geni gone off somewhere?"

"She's taking a landscape watercolor class," the boy responded, his mood improved now that his eagle friend had arrived. "As for me, I've tried gazillion different flies without a single nibble. I guess it's time to hike on home."

"Hmm. Can't remember what they're called—don't need flies myself—but my eagle eye tells me that the landscape is bursting with ants, beetles, and fuzzy-headed grasshoppers. All of them are insects that trout devour. Tried any that resemble those?"

The young fisherman knew something about these insects, too. In his fly-box, ready-to-go, was a *Fat Albert*, plump, juicy, and wiggly as a walrus. He had fished with a *Turk's Tarantula*, hard to identify the insect that it looks like, but the fish don't seem to care. He had heard of but never used an *Evil-eye Cricket*, a ground-dwelling "terrestrial" favored by skilled fishermen.

However, despite Mike Mulligan's advice, Nick decided some lunch might ease his frustration and possibly even change his luck. So, as the eagle flew off calling, "*See ya,*" the boy sat down under an aspen and took a peanut butter sandwich and a can of lemonade out of the large pocket in the back of his vest. He left the orange and the bag of Gummy Bears for later.

As he was eating, an unexpected thing happened. A sizeable grizzly bear came out of the woods, paused about eighty yards away, sniffed, and lumbered over to the river. He glanced at Nick once or twice without much interest, clearly having other things on his mind.

The two teens found the bears of the park almost as interesting as the wolves, at least from a distance. Moreover, when he first introduced Nick, and later Geni, to the magic berries, Mike had made sure that they understood, "You can only talk back and forth with the animals when you become one of them. But even then, you must be careful around bears, cougars, and wolves—they are always hungry, and always unpredictable."

As usual, Nick was careful to keep his distance, fully aware that this was not a cuddly Teddy. This was a handsome, honey-colored, shaggy-backed King-of-the-Forest. The Big Guy grinned, with his teeth exposed, as if to signal, "It is lunchtime and here is the most excellent fisherman in the park, on the bank of his favorite marine-cuisine stream."

Having clarified his superiority as a fisherman, at least to himself, the Big Guy entered the water with stealth and grace, so as not to scare the fish, and waded out into the riffles. Before Nick knew what had happened, the bear plunged his head under and emerged with a delicious-looking rainbow held firmly between his fangs.

As Nick continued to watch, he saw Bruno splash out of the stream, set his prize down on the shore, and lower his head to devour the scrumptious meal. Displaying the well-known grizzly appetite, the bear polished off the rainbow, licked his paws, turned, and waded back into the Madison for more.

The young angler was filled with a mix of conflicting emotions. He imagined recounting this bear fishing episode at the dinner table: "I admired his skill as a fisherman. But also, I was jealous that he caught a fish on his first try while I had not had a bite in three hours. Nevertheless, I was pleased to have a grizzly fish tale to bring home."

Chapter 17—Working Out a Deal

Soon, after moving to a spot a little deeper in the river, the bear's shaggy head went under water again. Then he rose, took a mighty leap, and came up with another rainbow clutched in his paws, this one even bigger and appearing more mouthwatering than the first. As he watched the grizzled angler carry his catch toward shore, an idea popped into Nick's head, resulting in a quick decision.

Reaching into his backpack, he lifted out the branch of magic berries, plucked one and swallowed it. *In the past, Mike had been with him at moments like this,* Nick thought, a little nervously, *so I wonder how it will turn out without him.*

In less than a minute, the boy realized that the change was happening. When he looked down at his feet, he saw talons, perfect for perching on a dead tree limb, or grasping a trout just below the surface of the stream.

"OMG! Am I becoming Mike Mulligan?"

At first, as the transformation continued, Nick believed that, yes, because of the size and brown coloring, he was becoming a bald eagle. But soon, catching sight of his reflection in the river, he realized that his beak was black and that there was a dark mask across the eyes of his white face. A bald eagle has a bright yellow beak and an entirely white face. Then, looking down again, he made out black not yellow talons that he found he could swivel in opposite directions. Finally, knowing that eagles had dark bodies—hadn't he seen Mike up close many times—he turned his head to the side and noticed much of his body was white.

"Uh-oh! I'm an osprey. Mike will be horrified!" he exclaimed, remembering the scene the eagle got into involving an osprey at the Beaver Olympics.

When the change was complete, he was two feet tall and six feet across the wings. Nick also knew that he had become an expert fisher-bird, whose vision enabled him to spot trout underwater from heights of 50 to 150 feet, and to firmly clutch a slippery fish with his reversible talons. But as adept an angler as he had become, Nick felt more than ever that he wanted no other fish than the gorgeous rainbow only eighty yards away.

The bear looked puzzled seeing an osprey glide toward him carrying a fishing vest in his claws. He lowered the big trout to the ground, wondering what this odd bird was up to. While hovering a few feet off the ground, Nick stuck a talon into a vest pocket and pulled out the orange. Hoping to strike a bargain, he held it out toward the bear and pointed a wing at the fish.

"Any chance you might want to trade that rainbow for this delicious orange?" he asked.

Thoughtfully, Brownie stared at the orange, then at the rainbow, and finally back at the osprey before shaking his shaggy head from side to side and responding, "NO DEAL."

However, Nick's longing to succeed in the trade had become so great that he reached into his food pocket again and brought out the Gummy Bears . . . obviously the perfect choice for Bruno. Believing that the Griz would be unable to resist this temptation, Nick held the *chewy irresistible* out toward the big guy.

"I bet you've never tasted anything as scrumptious as a Gummy Bear, so here's your chance. You'll wonder where it's been all your life."

Despite starting to sniff and drool, Bruno again shook his head and declared, "NO DEAL."

Nick was just about to give up and fly off toward home when suddenly the memory of a recent sighting struck him. If there is one thing a bear cannot resist, it's *honey,* and he knew where the HONEY was!

Once more, he focused his attention on the Griz with the perfect rainbow. "Don't move," he urged, "and don't gobble up that fish. I will be back in a flash with a reward so exciting you will believe bear Christmas has arrived five months early."

"Since you put it that way," the bear allowed, for whom Christmas was a special occasion, "what else can I do? But I can tell you, you are one strange osprey."

Nick flew back into the woods along his original path and in a few minutes, sure enough, hanging from a tree limb was the honeycomb, right where he expected to find it. In one graceful swoop, down he dove, grasped it carefully in his talons, gratified to see it dripping with sweet, mouthwatering nectar.

Back he zoomed, elated to find the fellow angler, *and the trout,* waiting right where he had left them. What a smart and curious bear he was to do what the osprey hoped he would do, strange bird or not. As the fish-hawk approached, the Big Guy stood up on his hind legs, raised his nose into the air, and sniffed louder than ever. In addition, the bear's grin was so broad Nick could hardly see the rest of his face.

85

This was the moment when Nick knew, for sure, that Bruno smelled something he really wanted—*HONEY!*

"Well, *Señor Oso*," Nick said, as he plunked the honeycomb down at the bear's feet, "are you finally ready for a trade?"

Without hesitating, the bear shoved the fish toward the osprey and, drooling politely, reached out and grasped the honeycomb. Nick picked up the rainbow, overjoyed that at the end of the day it was a done deal!

Before they went their separate ways, the two Madison River fisher-pros shared a few final words of praise.

"As a trader, Mr. Griz, you're a whiz!" the Bird-Boy observed.

Not to be outdone, the bear rose up to his impressive full height—at least eight feet, Nick the Osprey reckoned—smiled at the hovering raptor and acknowledged, "As a wheeler-dealer, Buddy-Bird, you surely have the muscle for the hustle."

As Nick watched the griz clump over a grassy knoll and fade into the distance, a worry crept back into his head. Not only had he never swallowed a magic berry when Mike wasn't on hand, but the eagle had always been there when he became a teen again. Perched on the limb of a fallen cottonwood watching the bear disappear, the osprey feared he hadn't fully thought through the situation.

But then out of nowhere a rocket shot past him almost knocking him off the branch. He ducked frantically when the missile came around for a second strike. This time, however, he had an inkling of what was happening. The third attempt was the clincher—it was Mike Mulligan once again showing his contempt for ospreys.

86

"Hey, you bird-brain," Nick shouted as the eagle zoomed by, "Mr. Franklin was right, the turkey should be the national bird, not some sky-diving goofball who doesn't realize how foolish he looks."

"Knew it was you the whole time," Mike Mulligan insisted, but instead of sticking around to win the argument, he called "Later," over his shoulder as he flew toward the orange and green sky visible behind Monument Mountain, 10,000 feet high in the Madison Range. In the next moment Nick had become his old teen self.

When Nick arrived home, his mother took one look at the trout and exclaimed, "What an awesome rainbow you've caught. What fly did you use?"

"Must have been a honey-scented *Terrestrial*," Nick replied, knowing she was familiar with most fly types and hoping his answer would be enough to satisfy her curiosity without having to reveal the whole tale.

In the evening, Nick was sitting alone on the porch when Geni wandered over and listened to his account of the day's adventure—*a short version*, she insisted. A few minutes later, Mike landed near him on the railing. "I still think you should have taken my advice about insects," the eagle stated, always eager to get credit for any success the boy may have had. "Anything would have been better than getting help from one of those featherheads who don't know a Long-nosed Sucker from a Utah Chub."

"There's more to the story than you know, but I suspect, since the trout has been grilled and consumed, you won't want to hear another of my fish tales at the end of such a nice day. I was just asking Geni how the watercolor class went."

"It was excellent" she stated, "except for the bobo eagle who insisted on posing in the very center of the scene we were painting."

The Alpha Female

Chapter 18—The Astonishing Encounter at the Rock Pile

In the early morning, a thick mist hovered over the meadow. When the teens came out of the trees into an open area, Nick saw something quite unusual. Visible just over the top of the undergrowth, a huge pair of antlers was poking out of the mist. They rose about three feet above the tall stalks of grass and, from point to point, were at least four feet across. It was instantly clear not only that the rack once belonged to a bull elk, but that he must have been enormous. Knowing that elk shed their antlers once every year, the boy was thrilled to imagine arriving home with such an elegant trophy.

"Got to have a closer look," Nick said to Geni as they walked together out into the meadow toward this remarkable sight. They hadn't gotten far when the antlers began to rise like a ghost out of the mist. Suddenly, the pair realized what was happening. Beneath the antlers, emerging from the undergrowth was perhaps the biggest elk they had ever seen, as alive as he could be. The tall grass had hidden everything but the antlers that were eerily visible through the haze. Now there he was at full height watching the boy and girl.

"Wow, Geni," Nick whispered, "isn't he magnificent?"

"*¡En verdad, Es magnifico!*" she quietly agreed, although her knees were shaking.

For an instant, Nick thought the elk might be ticked that they woke him up so early. But the boy quickly relaxed when this prince of forest nobility, raising his handsome head and rack, stepped majestically away from them into the woods.

The elk sighting should have been enough to make their day, Nick thought, but around midmorning, totally by chance, they made a discovery that took their breath away again. Walking at the edge of the woods, just where the treeline ended and the meadow fell sharply down into the valley below, they heard a little cry, a forlorn whimper. At first they couldn't find the location of the sound. But as the two friends searched and listened, they realized the noises were coming from a large pile of boulder-sized rocks. They climbed to the top, peered down into a small, deep hole, and were astonished to see a wolf pup trapped at the bottom staring unhappily up at them.

"How in the world did you get down there?" Geni wondered aloud.

The little lobo didn't know whether to be glad that *something* had finally found him, or scared because it was the unfamiliar sight, sound, and smell of humans. At first Nick, Geni, and the wolf pup just gazed at each other, all three uncertain what might happen next. Perhaps instinctively, the pup seemed to realize that the two teens were the only creatures around that could help him get out of this impossible situation. So the boy and girl settled on one of the rocks to look down on the little guy, hoping to come up with a plan to set him free.

Before long, Nick had an idea. He told Geni to keep a cautious eye peeled while he ran home for supplies. "But even safer if you move away from the rock pile while I'm gone," he advised. "It's quite possible that mother lobo will come looking for her missing pup."

A short time later, the boy returned with a large wooden bucket, a strong rope, and the secret ingredient . . . a scoop of raw

90

ground beef. First he tied the rope around the handle of the bucket, then squished a bit of meat on the bottom. Ready for the next step, he lowered the bucket down the hole and, when it reached the ground, let it slam against a stone hard enough to turn it on its side. All this activity made such a clatter that the frightened pup tried to crawl under a rock in the corner farthest from the pail. They could hear it whimper from its hiding place.

As they waited, they realized that the next step was up to the pup. Hunger would have to make him brave enough to come out from under the rock and get a whiff of the raw hamburger waiting for him at the bottom of the bucket.

A long time passed, maybe fifteen or twenty minutes. Again and again, they peered down into the hole, but no sign of the little guy. Finally, too impatient to wait any longer, Geni turned and asked, "Is there any meat left?"

When Nick handed her what there was, she squished half of the meat into a ball and tossed it down so that it rolled near the rock where the pup was hiding. In a few seconds, out came a small paw and grabbed it. Then Geni flattened the other half and dropped it at the mouth of the pail. Slowly and cautiously, the pup crept up to the meat and, in a flash, chomped it down.

At this very moment, a howl shattered the stillness. This was not the yip of a little furry puppy, but the deep-throated, all-business, spine-tingling howl of a full-grown wolf. Geni and Nick went rigid on top of the rock pile. The noise that made them freeze, however, instantly caused the pup to respond eagerly. Raising his head and twitching his ears, he yipped and yapped that this was a sound he recognized.

Later that day, when the two friends were mulling over this intriguing moment together, they realized, based on what happened next, how lucky they had been. However the pup may have understood the message in his mother's wolf call—perhaps it reminded him of her warmth when he was suckling—the little fellow became so excited that his appetite took charge. Whatever the explanation, he made a beeline into the bucket and immediately began to munch on the hamburger plastered against the bottom.

Quickly, Nick jerked on the rope and began to hoist the container with its upside-down passenger. When pail and cargo reached the mouth of the hole, he lifted them out and carried them down the rock pile onto the ground below. There, not wanting to touch the pup, whose wolf teeth he recalled were very sharp, Nick gently turned the bucket on its side. They watched the little lobo bravely crawl out, peering in every direction, a hunk of ground beef clinging to its nose.

Chapter 19—Namib, the Lovely Lobo

Nick was about to give Geni a round of applause for the successful strategy that lured the pup into the bucket, when the powerful howl rang out again. This time, as the teen twosome scrambled back to the top of the rock pile, the sound was only feet away. Of course the little guy heard the howl too, abruptly changed direction, and sped, tumbling head-over-heels in excitement, straight toward the source as fast as his short legs would carry him.

At the edge of the woods stood a strikingly beautiful female wolf. Her body was the color of thunderclouds, while her face, paws, and tail were lighter, almost white. The raven black ears and tip of her tail were the final perfect touches to her stunning image. If she had snarled, both teenagers would likely have dived into the hole the pup had just come out of. But she merely glanced their way, then turned her attention to the pup who was leaping up and licking her muzzle in a heartwarming display of *amor lobo* as Geni called it—wolf love. In a moment, the two wolves trotted side by side across the meadow and disappeared into the woods.

When the teens finished recounting the story to Nick's parents that night, Nick's father glanced at them and remarked, "I bet you just saved the life of the alpha female's pup. That was a pretty brave thing to have done."

"Alpha female?" Geni wanted to know. "*Que es* an alpha female?"

"It's a little like being *Queen Bee*," Nick's Dad answered. "Each wolf pack has an alpha female. She's the most important female in the pack, sometimes even more powerful than the alpha male. She rules the roost and calls the shots—no one wants to tangle with her."

"Once I heard the howl and realized how near she was, I'm not sure I'd have *tangled* with lobo royalty or *el hombre pequeño*, the little fellow," Geni reacted thoughtfully."

On an afternoon several weeks later, the two friends hiked near the meadow where they had seen the huge elk. It was such a cold day that they not only wore warm jackets, but stuck gloves and hats into their backpacks as well. That would soon prove to be good thinking on their part. They wandered for a couple of hours without seeing anything much—white pelicans and other waterbirds on the Yellowstone River were the most interesting.

"It's always intriguing to come upon white pelicans, partly because they are so distinctive, combining size and weirdness—long beaks, large throat pouches, and six-foot wing spans," explained Nick. Then he told Geni about the amazing experience a year ago when, thanks to Mike Mulligan and the magic berries, he and the other wolf pups rode pelican-back across a pool in the Lamar River.

But then, suddenly and without warning, the weather changed. The sky grew dark and a howling wind began to blow storm clouds above the meadow and across the river valley. When the first flakes of snow started to fall, Nick realized that they were about to be caught in the middle of a summer blizzard. As it got colder, the snow fell harder, and the gusting wind made the flakes whirl wildly, causing everything to go white. Nick had been in white-outs before in the mountains of Colorado, but never in Yellowstone Park and never far from shelter. Having spent most of her life in Madrid and Barcelona, where snowfall was rare, Geni had never known a blizzard.

Both teens put on their hats and gloves to keep warm, but that wouldn't help them find the way home. After wandering blindly for several minutes, Nick knew and Geni suspected that they were lost.

"We have to make a choice now," Nick said to Geni. We can continue groping our way through the storm, hoping to head in the right direction, or hang here until the storm ends."

"I have never been in such *mal tiempo,* unfriendly weather, but you have, so tell me what you think is best and then *I'll make the decision,*" she announced with a wink, followed by a sly grin that she made no effort to hide.

Nick understood that despite her playful words, she trusted him to make the right call, given his greater experience in the western wilderness. Despite the sudden drop in temperature and the blast of snow, her trust warmed him, but it also made him feel responsible for their safety. The harder he thought about what to do, the harder it snowed, almost impossible now to see their fingertips.

But before he could make up his mind, an extraordinary thing happened. They heard a howl, not far away, unmistakably the howl of a wolf. They stopped, waited, and listened. Then a second howl, this time closer. A moment later, even with the poor visibility, they could make out a gray object with a white face moving toward them through the white-out. As she came to a halt only a few feet away, they both realized.it was the *alpha female,* the mother of the pup the teens had rescued from the hole beneath the rock pile.

Because of the way she looked at them, pausing often as if to make sure the two humans were paying attention, Nick and Geni decided maybe, just possibly, she wanted them to follow her. And so they did. Ten minutes later they came to a sheltered area in the forest

95

where the wind was not so fierce, where it became easier to see beyond their mittens through the heavy snow. There, right before them, was the wolf pup's rock pile. As they approached, the splendid creature emitted a soft growl, gave Nick and Geni one last intense look, and loped away

Just then, the boy and girl heard a familiar flapping of wings.

"Strange weather for you two to be out for a stroll," called Mike Mulligan. "As for myself, well, even a hardy, well-insulated *leucocephalus* like me would prefer to curl up like a tabby in front of the fire rather than suffer frozen feathers in a snowstorm like this!"

The teens stared at each other, their faces scrunched in puzzled expressions. "*Loco-what?*" they uttered in the same breath.

"Well, speaking as a *homo sapiens*, I fear you have finally gone off the deep end, old buddy," Nick observed.

"Exactly where were you keeping warm during this perilous chapter in our lives that we only survived by a whisker, a wolf whisker that is?" Geni asked the eagle.

"We won't worry about the accuracy of *perilous*," Mike Mulligan replied lightheartedly, but was clearly much relieved to have found his wandering teenagers. "We'll just be thankful that the lovely lobo—called *Namib*, meaning 'Star-Dancer'—recognized the humans in trouble were the ones who saved her pup. Otherwise, I'd still be out there for who knows how much longer searching for you. Now Nicholas, would you kindly brush the snow off my wings—no de-icers here in the park, you know."

Grateful but not surprised to learn of the raptor's concern, Nick grabbed his hat and swept an inch of powder from his friend's back. Then he suggested that the raptor fly along with them to his family's cabin, where the trio could warm up together in front of the fire he would quickly build in the fireplace.

"How about I do fire, you do *el chocolate caliente*," she growled.

"You can even listen to the whole amazing story, beginning to end, when we tell it to our moms and dads. Remember to button your beak to keep secret that we can talk to each other. As a reward," he went on, "you can try a sip of my hot chocolate."

"I'll pass on the hot choc," the eagle choked, "but if you have a bit of that buffalo jerky you were handing out the other day . . . now that is an entirely different proposition"

Soon they were home, happy and snug in a familiar place out of the storm. Moments later, after the four parents had arrived from the ranger station, much relieved, Nick and Geni shared the details of the day's extraordinary adventure.

Later, annoyed that because of the adults he was forced to keep his beak shut, Mike had flown off in search of something fit for raptor consumption. But the conversation about the amazing events of the day continued.

"Is it possible," Nick wondered, "that the wolf helped us find the way through the blizzard because she actually remembered that we had rescued her pup?"

"Although it may sound strange," his mother answered, "wolves, like dogs, can have a sense of recognition and even affection for human beings. Also, I believe both breeds have good memories. But the wonderful thing is," offering the last word on the subject, "that the wolf was there to help you in the snowstorm, and Mike Mulligan arrived to guide you home."

"We know that wolves and some dogs look a lot alike, so maybe they are similar in other ways," Geni agreed. "What's more, I think the pup would have come to help, if it had been a little older. Well anyway," she added, "whatever the explanation, I'm glad the alpha female arrived when she did. Who knows when that *pollo perezoso*, that lazy chicken, would have shown up," she affectionately teased the absent eagle.

The *Eager* Bachelor Beaver

Chapter 20—Building the Dam Comes First

During this second wonderful Yellowstone summer, Nick was fly-fishing one of the small streams, Elk Tongue Creek, which flowed through Slough Creek into the Lamar River. He had just caught a nice cutthroat trout on a #14 Olive Dun—and returned it to the water—when he came upon a beaver dam. Although he had seen them up close before, this one drew his special attention. The green freshness of tree trunks and branches told him that the dam was new; and the fact that the small creek still rushed downstream indicated that the beaver's work was unfinished. But just then, Nick heard his stomach growling that it was lunchtime.

So he sat down on an old cottonwood log, opened his backpack, and began to munch on a tuna sandwich. The sky was blue, the sun was warm, and a gentle breeze kept the temperature at just the right level. As Nick happily enjoyed another beautiful day in the park, Mike Mulligan landed with a plunk beside his friend.

"Now that you're here," were the raptor's first words, "the only thing that will make life better is Geni's return."

"She and her parents are spending several days in Cody, just outside the park, but she should be back tomorrow," Nick replied.

"Well okay, but lunchtime for you means lunchtime for me. Back soon," as the eagle lifted off into the blue.

After chomping down his sandwich, Nick decided to save the apple and Snickers bar for later. As he was about to pick up his fly rod and amble over to the pool he had been fishing, he saw something

99

moving. There, scuttling along the unfinished dam, was the beaver himself dragging the trunk of a young aspen, bark gone and branches pretty well stripped. Nick's dad had told him beavers must be alert whenever they cut down a tree so that it doesn't topple onto them, adding that a smart beaver knows which way to skedaddle the instant the tree begins to fall.

The boy watched as the busy builder lay the trunk carefully across the opening between the left and right sides of the dam, then returned to shore for another small tree soon to be placed in the same spot. Then another and another.

It was easy to get a good view of the beaver when he paused to look over and approve his work. Nick judged him to be a young male, full grown and healthy. He had always found the beaver a fascinating animal and had, from time to time, come across articles about them in nature magazines. So whenever he had the chance, he'd sit down, as he did now, to check out the industrious creature at work.

During Nick's first summer in the park—talking to rangers, naturalists and others—he learned that beavers, along with squirrels, mice, and porcupines, were Yellowstone rodents, and all have strong, sharp teeth for gnawing. (Having once spent the day as a porcupine, thanks to a magic berry, Nick knew something about rodent behavior.) A beaver's front teeth are not only intended for eating berries, grass, and water plants, but also for use where needed most—to eat bark, roots, twigs, and fresh leaves of trees. However, they use the tree itself to build dams and homes. Wildlife experts refer to the beaver, the largest rodent in North America, as *Castor canadensis*, Nick recalled reading somewhere.

(When he offered to explain to Geni what the Latin words meant, she sniffed, "*Un momento*, Bobo, *castor* also happens to mean 'beaver' in Spanish."

"Well then," he grinned, "I'm sure you can deal with *canadensis* on your own.")

Nick had also come to know that a beaver's life can be tricky. In the streams and rivers, they are safe because they are excellent swimmers. Their webbed rear feet and broad tail enable them to speed through the water. The fact that they can stay under water for as long as fifteen minutes is a real bonus when it comes to safety. But on land, where they must find trees for building projects and for most of their food, there can be danger because they can only plod along slowly. A hungry wolf is not the only predator who considers the beaver a treat. Others, including coyotes, lynx, wolverines, and even black or brown bears occasionally regard the beaver as a particularly appetizing meal.

To survive, a beaver must choose a place in the stream where the current isn't too strong and where food is plentiful. Then, to slow down the current and deepen the water, he builds a dam—just what Nick's beaver was doing right now. Eventually, the dammed-up high water protects him from predators, who prefer to steer clear of a chilly deepwater bath.

This beaver began his project by gnawing branches and sticks and, with strong front paws, poking them into the mud on the river-bottom. Next came small-ish tree trunks, followed by more sticks pushed in between the trunks. The beaver-builder repeats the process until, satisfied with the structure, he makes it sturdy and watertight by shoving mud and earth and leaves in among the sticks.

Nick watched him working his way, little by little, across the stream, keeping the top of the dam above the water level as he labored. The more mud and stones he pushed between the branches, the more the water was blocked from flowing through. And the harder he toiled, the more interested Nick became. In fact, he returned for several days to keep an eye on the energetic builder until finally the two sides of the dam were joined and the water, almost completely blocked, began to back up to form a pond. Nick estimated the dam to be 100 feet wide—some dams, he had heard, were as wide as the length of a football field. At this point he was excited to show Geni, knowing that she would find nature's skilled engineer as fascinating as he did.

As the beaver took a breather to survey his handiwork, Nick could tell that he was proud of what he had accomplished so far. Not only had the dam created the necessary pond, but nearby was a grove of young aspen that, without making the beaver travel far from the safety of the river, would provide food, as well as wood for the second project.

Nick knew that once the dam was finished, the beaver would start on his home, work that Nick wouldn't easily see from the riverbank. But he hoped to find a book or magazine that would include pictures and descriptions of a beaver house.

At that very moment, the river dweller dove into the pond, whacking the surface with his tail as he went under. The smack was so loud that Nick leapt off the log he was sitting on and peered up and down the far bank, knowing that beavers do this to warn others of danger, a warning that might be heard more than a half mile away.

Sure enough, a coyote had rushed to the edge of the stream and was standing on the bank, staring at the circle in the water where the beaver had disappeared. Beavers know that predators cannot catch them in deep water—only river otters, as much at home in the water as beavers themselves, remain a threat. But the otter's favorite foods include, first and foremost, fish—perch and suckers—as well as frogs, turtles and snails, so attacks on bigger, stronger beavers are rare. The frustrated coyote continued to look intently at the spot where he had last seen the beaver, then turned and stalked off into the woods to search elsewhere for lunch.

Three days later, Nick returned with Geni. Eager to introduce her to "my eager beaver," as he now called him, he had shared with her his new familiarity with dam-building and was deep into a description of underwater home construction as they arrived at the stream.

"But isn't it *arriesgado* not to have a hiding place until the house is finished," she wondered?

"If I'm right that *arriesgado* means 'unsafe' I think I can explain." Around Geni, Nick tried hard to remember his Spanish. "While Señor Castor is busy building his new home—called *a lodge,* incidentally—he lives in a *bank burrow,* a hole scooped out along the edge of the stream. He is quite safe there until he puts the final touches on his *casa elegante.*"

As they settled down on the cottonwood log to share a snack and watch the master builder at work, Geni smiled at Nick, "Your *fluidez en Español* is also *elegante,* although 'risky' is a better way to translate *arriesgado.*"

Chapter 21—Next Comes *la Casa Elegante*

Now that the dam was completed, its most important purpose became clear. Before the beaver can build his lodge, the pond must be deep enough to construct a mound from the riverbottom up. Sometimes the mound will be placed in the middle and other times near the shore. This beaver decided to locate in the middle.

As the boy and girl sat there admiring the builder's skill, they wondered how he planned to get in and out of his lodge. To get a better look, they knelt down on hands and knees at the section of the pond nearest his worksite. Unfortunately, the water wasn't clear enough to see the details of the beaver's still-under-construction dwelling.

At this moment, Mike Mulligan landed beside them. "Been occupied, some miles away," he reported, "watching a young bald eagle dive into the Yellowstone River. Gave the fledgling a few important pointers," he added. Then, noticing that both the teens' chins were dripping wet, commented, "Looks as if the two of you may also need diving instruction from an expert."

Wiping the water from her face, Geni looked over at him, "And I am glad to see you, too, you *halcón del pollo tonto*, you silly chicken hawk. I've truly missed you!"

Doing his best to look offended, Mike covered his face with a wing and mumbled a reply that neither teen-ager could decipher. But quickly hitting upon the perfect retort, he fastened an eagle eye on Geni.

"Not surprising," he declared, "that earthbound humans are envious of those who soar above them!"

"Maybe you can help us bone up on those who swim beneath us," Nick chimed in. "After all, the beaver is nature's *numero uno* architect. At the moment, he is working too far under water to get a clear picture."

"Lucky for you, I just may have the solution," was the raptor's thoughtful reply. "Got the magic berries?"

Nick removed the branch from his backpack, plucked two berries and, as he swallowed one, Geni did the same. Then they watched each other become smaller and smaller, all the way down to about seventeen inches in length. They noticed coats of thick brown fur beginning to wrap their bodies, and new tails, flat and covered with scales, that were so long they dragged on the ground.

"Why the flat tails?" Geni wanted to know.

"I bet we learn why pretty soon," was Nick's prediction.

"Okay, but in the meantime, what exactly have I just become?"

"A muskrat," came Nick's answer, "and almost as cute as a marine iguana."

"And what kind of rat did you say you were, if I may ask?" she countered, unaware that muskrats happen not to be members of the rat family.

Nick remembered from somewhere that the name comes from the "musky" odor—*strong and pungent*—created when the animal marks its territory. The muskrat shares the freshwater streams of

105

Yellowstone with other *semiaquatic* mammals, the river otter, for example, and of course the beaver now laboring on his lodge right in front of them. Like the beavers, the muskrats' front paws are designed for digging tunnels and constructing homes that provide safety and shelter.

"I'm particularly impressed by your swimsuits," Mike Mulligan offered. "Yours I assume is from Orvis, Geni? Nick's from a garage sale in Gardiner, Montana, perhaps?"

Ignoring the eagle's feeble attempt at humor, the two new muskrats skittered off toward the stream and slithered into the water. With barely a ripple, they sank toward the bottom before stroking free-style across the stream. They were amazed how their thick fur kept them warm despite the chilly temperature of Elk Tongue Creek. But what astonished them occurred when they kicked their webbed feet and, even more, when they flicked their flat tails. They shot through the water like miniature atomic submarines, arriving at the far bank in seconds.

"Wow," Nick bubbled, his breath emitting a stream of underwater bubbles, "we are certainly a pair of rapid rodents."

"When's the next Summer Olympics?" Geni burbled back.

"I doubt muskrats are eligible," Nick gurgled in return.

Then, reversing direction, they glided toward the mound on which the beaver had built his lodge. And there he was, hard at work, putting the finishing touches on the underwater tunnels, the only entrances or exits to his new dwelling.

"Nothing could get in that *casa* no matter how hungry—not a wolf, a lynx, or even a bear— *nunca nada jamás*," Geni observed, full of admiration for the beaver's skill. "His family will be totally safe in there."

"He surely is a great home designer," Nick agreed, "but I wish we could see what it looks like inside."

"Me, too," said Geni. "Maybe we could coax an invitation."

As the muskrat pair approached the new dome-home, they noticed that the same materials had been used in the construction of the dam. They saw, as expected, that the mound was about ten feet high and twenty feet wide at the bottom.

"It looks like the Native American *wigwam*s that we just saw at the Plains Indian Museum in Cody," Geni observed. "I learned that they are also called *wickiups* and *wecus*."

Just as they were circling the structure looking for a way to get inside, the builder himself, flapping his broad tail like a paddle, came cruising by. Without a glance in their direction, he sped past and disappeared into a tunnel well below the surface of the creek.

"Wait up," Nick warbled after him, "we were hoping for a tour of your elegant new home." But it was too late.

"What now?" Geni gurgled. "And incidentally, do we know how beavers feel about muskrats?"

"I guess, sooner or later, we're likely to find out," as he poked his fuzzy nose into the tunnel. "I hope he's in a generous mood," at which point Nick disappeared as suddenly as the beaver.

"¿*Que pasó* ? What just happened?" Geni squalled. "¿*Dónde estás?* Where are you?"

Chapter 22—Muskrats Are Welcome!

No sooner had she expressed her puzzlement, when a muskrat paw emerged from the lodge and presented what was unmistakably a *"c'mon in"* signal.

She entered the tunnel only to find herself climbing up and up until she burst into a cozy, dry room. There, eagerly awaiting her arrival, were two particularly cute rodents.

"Welcome, muskrat princess," said the bigger one.

"Geni, this is Tukk. Tukk, this is Geni." The smaller one made the introductions before continuing, "He is *beaver-ish* to show us around his *bee-oo-tee-ful* new home."

"Don't you mean *fever-ish?*" the female muskrat corrected.

"Whatever," was the other muskrat's reply, disappointed that the word he had just invented and considered witty hadn't sparked a single chuckle.

"Pleased to meet you, Geni," said Tukk.

"*Encantada también,* Tukk. Seeing your home will be a real treat. But first, out of curiosity, would you tell me how you got such an unusual name."

"Actually, it's a question I'm often asked. The name is short for *Tukkuttok,* which means "generous" in the Inuit language. I was named after Grandfather Beaver, who immigrated from Alaska years before I was born."

"How wonderful. Nick was hoping you'd be *generous*—and you are!"

"Let's begin the tour from the beginning—the building of the all-important mound," Tukk suggested, eager to show off his handiwork. "First I start by poking sticks into the mud at the bottom of the pond to form the foundation."

"On top of the foundation comes a structure made of more sticks, bark, rocks, grass, leaves, plants, and anything else available, all plastered together with mud. It is shaped like a dome and extends upward until it is several feet above the surface of the stream. At this point it is solid through and through, with no entrance or open space inside.

"Once completed, I start chewing and clawing and digging to hollow out two entrance tunnels and two rooms. I'll show you the tunnels first."

Back down went the trio, stopping where the tunnel opened into the pond.

"The entry passages have to be well under the water level, to keep us safe from unwelcome visitors," Tukk explained. "In summer, most land prowlers will do anything to avoid *a shiver in the river*, especially when it's deep enough to force them to swim and even dive. But winter presents a different problem. Starting in the fall, I have to plaster the section of the dome that pokes out above the stream with fresh mud."

"That sounds like a lot of work just to prepare for winter when everything around is going to be wrapped in snow and ice," Geni observed. "And won't the pond be frozen?"

"Exactly!" boomed the beaver. "Because food is scarce during the cold months, the hungry predators will walk across a frozen pond to the visible part of the dome hoping to find something to eat."

"What will the mud coating accomplish?" Nick wondered. "I can't see a coyote or fox able to dig through it, but how about a powerhouse like a wolverine?"

"Think about it," Tukk encouraged the muskrats, still rather wet behind the ears when it came to understanding predator behavior. "When the temperature drops, it gets *reallllly cold* in Yellowstone. By early December, the mud freezes and the mound becomes as hard as granite. No animal, not even the mighty wolverine, can penetrate the walls of my fortress, though they will prowl across the ice and sniff around a bit."

"How do you feel about us, about muskrats, that is?" was the question Nick had been burning to ask. "Can't they come and go as easily as we did?"

"It may surprise you to know," Tukk answered, "muskrats and beavers get along so well that from time to time they live together in the same lodge."

Pleased to learn of this amiable rodent relationship, they followed Tukkuttok, back to the lower room.

Once there, Muskrat Nick gazed all around before asking, "Why do you need two rooms? Does each have a different purpose?"

"Absolutely," the beaver replied. "Can you guess how the lower room is used?'

"As the main entrance to the lodge?"

"Right on. First, it is the place we dry off after coming in from the stream. But also, it is where we store and eat the green wood bark collected in the fall and stuck into crevices in the wall. It stays cold, fresh, and available—a safe source of food all winter long."

"So we could call it a combination mudroom and dining room," Geni remarked.

"You got it," Tukk confirmed, as he led the way up to the second floor. "Finally, here is the living-sleeping-family room. Look up there," he gestured toward the ceiling. "One of the last lodge-building tasks is to make a hole too small for critters, but big enough for fresh air to flow. It is where we spend much of our time, especially during the cold months, and it is where we care for the little ones, *the kits*."

"It's a large room," Nick observed. "How many beavers will live here with you?"

Something about the question caused Tukk to pause before answering. The muskrats glanced at each other, realizing that for a few seconds their new friend seemed quietly lost in thought.

When he spoke, his voice had a quaver that hadn't been there before. "Well . . . ah . . . there are usually two to four adults and eight or more kits born over several seasons. Just haven't found the right Missus yet, I guess"

A week later, the teens returned to eat magic berries and once more shape-shift into muskrats. Though they had no idea how he did it, it had become apparent that Mike Mulligan was able to determine which animal they turned into after swallowing a magic berry. They swam underwater to the tunnel, carefully inspected the entire lodge, found everything completed and in perfect order—but no beaver.

"Where is Tukk?" Geni wanted to know.

"Having finished all his projects, perhaps he's floating in the pond, or paddling around upstream," Nick suggested. "In any case, let's cruise the creek and take a look."

Settled lazily on a dead tree stump, Mike Mulligan was waiting for them when they returned. His presence pleased them, each in a different way—Nick because of the remarkable history of their unique relationship; Geni who enjoyed not only the eagle's special friendship but also the condition they shared of *always being hungry*.

In fact, Nick found himself puzzling for the umpteenth time since they first met on the Lamar a year ago, *I don't know how anyone forever famished can always look so good, so slim and trim and healthy.*

"*¡Estoy hambriento!* I'm starving!" she confirmed the point. "So what does a muskrat eat?"

"Pond vegetation," Nick answered. "Waterlilies and cattails would be my guess."

"Pond critters, frogs, and crayfish, get my vote," was the raptor's opinion, influenced by his own ever-ravenous appetite.

At that very moment, a blur of bright colors—long yellow legs and a body covered with red hairs—came fluttering by. Unable to control her feeding frenzy, Geni leapt off the ground and appeared to

113

inhale the insect in midair. The instant she hit the ground, the morsel exploded from her mouth with a loud, "Ptooey!"

"Yech! *¿Qué fue?*" Geni exclaimed. "What was that??"

"I believe it was once a Tiger Moth," declared the eagle, "but quite recently it became a *ptooey.*"

"Sometimes you are as bobo as he is," she nodded in Nick's direction.

Hungrier than ever, as Geni's gaze lingered on Nicholas Muskrat, a recent memory resurfaced.

"Oh, Lord of Lamar, I have four important questions," she announced. "First, where is your backpack? Second, did we not bring cucumber sandwiches for lunch? Third, wouldn't a muskrat find a cucumber sandwich every bit as scrumptious as a waterlily? And last, didn't you hear my internal alarm system strike *lunchtime?*"

"Backpack on tree; sandwiches in backpack; river rodents relish *pepinos.*" His final remark, "food alarm *always* ringing," was lost on Genevieve Muskrat as she clambered speedily up the tree trunk to retrieve the food pack. In no time at all, they shared a sandwich confirming that muskrats, like certain teens, considered cucumbers a delicacy.

Chapter 23—Meeting the Menacing Mink, *Head On*

While they were keeping an eye out for Tukk, Mike Mulligan flew off to check on the diving progress of his eagle novices. "Back in a flash," he chirred as he disappeared over Specimen Ridge.

"Let's have another look in the lodge," Nick suggested, "in case our beaver buddy returned while we were distracted by lunchtime."

"I guess so," Geni agreed, "but I doubt he would have *whooshed* by us without shouting *hola, raton almizclero*—'howdy muskrats'—or something.

They swam out anyway, searched the lodge, and started to head to shore, still wondering what had become of Tukkuttok. They were halfway back *when it happened*.

At first it was a ripple on the surface of the pond, unusual because it was a calm windless day. But then Geni was bumped sharply from behind by a dark brown object almost twice her size. That it appeared to be driving her toward a shallow part of the stream became certain when it struck her again, this time with greater force.

Aware, as he cruised along several feet behind Geni, that they were suddenly facing an unidentified threat, Nick dove down to get a better view of the situation. What he saw made him quake like an aspen leaf. Propelling the female muskrat toward the riverbank was a long slim body with a bushy tail and short stubby legs. Its streamlined shape, water-shedding fur, and webbed feet enabled it to cruise speedily through the stream. With the speed and strength of a ten-pound brown trout, the critter was so at home in the pond that it out-maneuvered Geni every whichway she turned.

But it wasn't a trout. In fact, as Nick quickly grasped, it wasn't even a fish. Nor was it the river otter that he momentarily suspected. Sudden recognition sent shivers up and down his spine when he recalled that *muskrat* was one of this water-weasel's favorite foods. It was a mink!

Nick gulped, shuddered, pulled himself together and shot past Geni and her pursuer just as all three reached the shallow spot and became visible to each other.

"Back off, buster," the mink warned, "unless you're wacky enough to want to join the other one for lunch . . . my lunch, that is."

"You're the one that better watch out. This muskrat doubles team might have more lunch punch than you can handle," Nick countered, but without much confidence.

"*Heh, heh, heh*, quite the comedian," snickered the mink, totally unimpressed. "Two m'rats may delay my midday meal by a minute or two, but lunch will surely be served, and sooner than you can imagine."

"Well then, how about a pair of m'rats *plus one powerful and ravenous bald eagle*?" Nick quizzed, having caught sight of Mike Mulligan landing near them, a few feet from the edge of the stream. "Perhaps the moment has come for you to reconsider the menu."

"Can't believe how quickly a raptor on the radar screen can dull one's appetite," the mink glumly conceded, as it crept into the water and hurriedly disappeared.

Bursting with relief, Nick kept a careful eye on the muskrat girl, still shaking, as she crawled up onto dry land and collapsed at the foot of the tree that once held the backpacks. The muskrat boy followed slowly, aware that his heartbeat, pounding a moment ago, was returning to normal.

"In Spain," she gasped, "everyone understands that the excitement level during *fútbol* ("soccer" to you) goes ballistic when FC Barça beats Real Madrid in overtime. What happens in the U.S. when one barely avoids being lunch munch for a mink by luck and a whisker?"

"Ah, Geni," Mike offered, springing onto his tree stump, "don't put down your brave defender, or the *ready-for-action* presence of your winged guardian with the eagle eye."

Appreciating the truth in what the raptor said, she smiled shakily, but in a friendly way at her fellow muskrat, and then at their feathered friend. *"Está bien,* my fearless protector, I name you *héroe del día,* 'hero of the day.' And as for you, Señor Mulligan, your eagle eye certainly brought about your rapid return just when we needed you . . . *¡urgentemente!."*

Hero of the Day, especially noted in Spanish, was a bit much for Nick's natural modesty. Hoping to create a distraction, he vanished into the backpack and emerged with the remaining cucumber sandwich. In no time at all, Geni had devoured her half and most of his. But then, familiar with the way excitement affected her appetite, and especially sensitive to what she had just been through, Nick did not protest.

Chapter 24—Princess Yuka, the *Bright Star*

As she was licking the crumbs from her whiskers, Geni's thoughts took her back to what they were doing before the mink attack.

"In a little while, the sun will be setting behind Buffalo Plateau. There is no sign of Tukk, so maybe it's time for us to become humans again before *la mala*, the bad one, returns for another crack at dinner."

"I still can't imagine where Tukk has gone. Having put the finishing touches on his fabulous new home, what might cause him to wander off without a word?" Nick puzzled. "A vacation after all his hard work? I doubt it. A visit to other beavers? Wait a minute . . . what other beavers?"

In all the days they had spent there, they never saw another beaver in or near the pond. In fact, the last hour they had been with Tukk, he had spent most of it swimming round and round in the water, raising his head and looking upstream and down, above the dam and below, as if expecting someone.

It had made the teens a little sad when they recognized what looked like a down-in-the-dumps expression on his beaver face. They couldn't imagine why he should be gloomy, given everything he had accomplished.

But, as they stood at the water's edge considering the matter, Nick and Geni realized that what the lodge builder had in mind was neither a vacation nor some kind of beaver entertainment. "Isn't it true that when the lodge is ready, it means the time has come for the beaver to seek a mate and raise a family? His inability, so far, to find a female beaver is making him *muy triste*, very sad," said Geni.

Nick didn't mention it to Geni, but he had begun to worry that one of the predators might have snared Tukk when he ventured too far from the pond.

Then, just as sunset began to color the western sky, the two muskrats caught sight of a beaver head sticking out of the water some distance up the creek. Looking more intently, they felt a rush of hope as they made out not one, but two beavers swimming together toward the pond.

They recognized Tukkuttok leading the way, while glancing behind himself every moment or two to make sure he was still being followed. Once, when he realized he was too far ahead, he turned around and paddled upstream until the new beaver joined him to swim along side by side.

Before the beaver couple reached the pond, Tukk's gaze focused on the familiar muskrats who were keenly watching them approach. He saw the pair slip into the stream one final time and glide over to greet them. When the beaver twosome had entered the slower, deeper water, Tukk raised a paw and called out, "Gimme five!" to his m'rat buddies.

Then all four river rodents, in a water-dance of joy, did loops and leaps and somersaults together, grinning from furry ear to ear.

"Geni, Nick, this is *Yuka*—her name means Bright Star and, as Geni will be pleased to know, her grandparents were Inuit," he added proudly, "same as mine."

119

Then the skillful builder, puffing with pride, paused to be sure Yuka approved the beautiful new lodge. Causing barely a ripple, the pair plunged into their underwater palace. Nick and Geni didn't see the fetching female again that day, but their beaver buddy came to the surface a little while later, paddled to shore where he swiftly cut down a small leafy aspen and dragged it across the pond in the direction of the lodge.

As the teens, humans once more, headed for home, Nick commented, "I can't be sure, but I believe Tukk turned and winked at us just before he dove under with a tasty aspen treat for his new companion."

"My eagle-eye can confirm that," the handsome bald eagle declared, hovering a few feet overhead. "But did you know that beavers live for twelve to fifteen years and stay with the same mate for all the years of their lives?"

The Looniest Yellowstone Story . . . So Far

Chapter 25—Thunderclouds over Yellowstone

For the next few days following their beaver adventure, Nick and Geni could talk about little else. Never during the months they spent together in Yellowstone had an adventure included such highs and lows. On the low side (very low!), Muskrat-Geni, threatened by a mink, remained a vivid memory; on the high, they were still celebrating Tukk's return to his lodge with Yuka, his new *bright star.*

But no surprise, soon they were ready for new excitement.

Geni and Nick agreed to meet at the park bus stop near both of their cabins with fly-fishing gear and everything needed for a day on the stream. The plan was to fish the Gibbon River, which flowed near Norris Geyser Basin, not too far from Canyon Village. The fishing wasn't as good as in the Lamar or Slough Creek. But they always enjoyed seeing the herds of bison and elk grazing in the open fields on either side of the stream.

Nick wore the usual stuff—shorts and old sneakers for wading—and carried a backpack brimful of flies, extra tippet and clippers, along with snacks, water, and, of course, the branch of magic berries, just in case. Geni was dressed in her trendy fishing outfit— waders, boots, and an elegant vest loaded with every manner of equipment, most of which, her fellow fisherman was convinced, she would never use. But by then he had known and liked her long enough to accept her peculiarities, just as she accepted his . . . *he hoped.* For example, he didn't even comment when he saw that she had a new net dangling from a strap on her vest that was big enough to land a whale!

And Geni, as a favor to him, stuck to Spanish II vocab except when, occasionally, excitement caused her to use words he still hadn't learned. Nick continued to be impressed (and slightly envious, too) that she was bilingual. But in his mind he made up for it, at least a little, knowing he was the more experienced fisherman and *explorer of wild things and places,* and especially by knowing that he was *the keeper of the magic berries.*

The elk and bison came into view where the two fishermen had often spotted them, grazing peacefully in the meadow between the forest and the stream. Several of the shaggy beasts lifted their huge heads to glance at the teens. But the majority, uninterested in the pair's presence, kept munching away. Ranger Heathmore had recently explained that the words *bison* and *buffalo* were so commonly exchanged that either one had become okay, although "bison" was the scientifically correct name.

The young anglers reached their favorite fishing spot on the Gibbon, assembled rods and reels, and mulled over their fly collections. Each hoped to select the fly that would prove *irresistible* to the biggest trout lurking in the river's best pools. When they first fished together a year ago, Geni was an enthusiastic beginner. Soon she began to understand the skills of knowing where trout lurk, of smooth and accurate casting, and especially of fly selection. These topics, once deep dark secrets that neither would have dreamed of sharing freely with the other, were now regular topics of streamside conversations. However, even though they had become friends, the passion to win the fishing competition remained intense every time they dropped a fly onto park waters. Still, Nick couldn't help sneaking a peek to learn what Geni was tying onto the tippet. A split second later, he realized that had been a mistake.

"*¡Chalado!* You dingbat!" she shrieked. "I see you spying on my fly. Hah! That can only mean you are in a panic about picking the wrong one, *¿Tengo razón, Señor?* Am I right, Mister?"

"Just your imagination working overtime," he replied calmly, as he tied an *Adams Irresistible* fly to his line. "I already knew that you would choose a humongous creepy-crawly of Scottish design created to catch the Loch Ness monster."

With this little skirmish behind them, they settled down to their normal rivalry. Whoever hooked the first trout, the biggest trout, and the last trout of the day would win the contest and the bragging rights—*and oh! did each of them want to be the winner!*

A short time later, as the teens cast flies out onto the Gibbon, both hoping against hope for a strike, they became aware that the weather was changing. What had begun as a perfect Wyoming blue sky morning was rapidly turning into a gray and blustery afternoon. Before either could claim the first bite, they heard the unmistakable booms of thunder and glimpsed flashes of lightning, as a typical Yellowstone thunderstorm came rolling in from the West.

"*Pongámonos a cubierta,*" Geni advised. "We better take cover or we will be soaked to the skin, for sure."

"Or even worse," Nick quickly added, concentrating on where to find shelter in the storm, "if the lightning strikes come closer."

"Do you know where we can go?" she wondered.

"There's a covered area back at the bus stop," he remembered. "If we hustle, it should only take a few minutes to get there."

Because Geni's stiff boots were not built for speed anywhere, but especially not on land, it took longer to get to the bus stop than Nick had expected. Still, they made it there moments before the sky turned dark and the downpour drenched everything around them. Although they felt pretty well protected, they jumped nervously every time lightning struck, holding their breaths as they waited for the next blast, and the next.

"OMG!" Geni exclaimed when the flash and boom seemed to occur at the same instant, "that crash almost knocked me out of my socks!"

Even though they had met only a year ago, Nick was impressed by how much Geni's English had improved. She still sputtered foreign words, usually when excited. But mostly she was able to come up with the right expression in English. *In fact, the storm had moved so close and grown so ferocious that it could have knocked my socks off too*, he thought, . . . *at least if I'd been wearing any.*

Chapter 26—Mike Mulligan, Eagle Scout on Alert

Cloudbursts in Yellowstone have a way of ending as suddenly as they begin. The sun did not reappear, but the rain let up, then stopped altogether, and the rumbles grew faint and far between until all the pair heard was an occasional crackle in the distance.

Just as they were ready to pick up their rods and head back to the stream, a feathery whirring sound, accompanied by an unmistakable eagle cry, caused the two fishermen to look upward.

"I believe a new storm-cloud has settled in above us," Nick jokingly commented. "But no," he continued, "not a weather-related commotion at all—why it's none other than Michael Mulligan."

Usually, when their eagle buddy flew in, he either landed on Nick's shoulder, on a nearby dead tree branch, or on the ground in front of them, making little attention-grabbing nods and hops before delivering his latest gossip tidbit or gem of wisdom. Today, however, without actually touching down, he turned, soared straight up 20 or 30 feet, and hovered for several seconds.

Finally, knowing that he had his friends' full attention, he glided to the top of a small hill, landed, and called down, "Come up here with me, *asap!*"

"*¡Vámanos!*" Geni urged, both teens recognizing the alarm in the raptor's voice.

It was easy for Nick to dash up the hill in sneakers while Geni plodded along in her boots and waders. When the boy reached the top, it took only an instant to grasp Mike's warning. "Quick, look off to the West," the eagle shrilled.

125

There, a short distance away, the boy spied a giant plume of black smoke and a towering column of red and yellow flame rising from the burning trees.

"Holy smokes!" Nick shouted, as Geni joined him on the hilltop, both recognizing how dangerously close the blaze was. "The lightning must have started a fire that is spreading toward the campground near the village."

For a few seconds, they stood there, wracking their brains for anything they could do to prevent the flames from turning into an inferno. In the meantime, Mike Mulligan had flown back to the place he first met them and, in a single lunge, scooped up the backpack in his talons. Returning to the hilltop, he dropped the bag at Nick's feet, shouting, "Swallow a berry, then listen, and I'll explain."

Only then did Nick begin to get an inkling of the eagle's purpose. He couldn't help wondering, *could this be the first time in history that a bald eagle produced a forest fire action plan*? He opened the backpack and pulled out the branch of magic berries, gave one to Geni and swallowed another himself.

In moments, while Mike Mulligan nodded his handsome white head in approval, the teens began to change. Nick watched in amazement as Geni's face became black, her nose and mouth pointed, her neck covered with thin black and white stripes, and on her back a black and white checkerboard. In her new form, she staggered forward on large webbed feet, shaking her wings to prevent her beak from stabbing a fuzzy caterpillar who was innocently crawling by. But it was the remarkable sound she made—*whee-ooo-quee, hoo-leee-lie-leee*—that unquestionably identified her as a *loon*, one of the most beautiful of the northern lake birds, whose call was eerie, long-lasting, and unique.

Busy admiring her remarkable transformation, Nick failed to notice his own dark gray feathers and long tail. It wasn't until Geni had commented on his pale face and how hooked and stubby his nose had become, that he lowered his head and eyes far enough to appreciate the yellow talons and very handsome, "if I do say so," bright red vest that he was wearing beneath his outstretched wings.

He was such a handsome raptor that Geni couldn't help bringing to mind the fourteen year-old he had been a moment ago, even taller and more suntanned than he had been last summer.

When the boy opened his mouth to request some admiration for the particularly stylish outfit, out came a scream and a whistle— *kweeaaaaah, pi tip, pi tip, pi tip*—as loud as any sound he'd ever heard a bird make. At that point he knew he was a hawk, though it wasn't clear until later what kind of hawk.

But that could wait—the immediate concern was that during the few minutes they had spent on the hilltop the blaze had crept much closer to the campground. When the threesome flew up to get a better view, they were shocked to see the prairie grass on fire near fifteen or twenty elk and a bison herd that easily numbered close to two hundred of the rain-soaked beasts.

As they hovered together above the flames, Mike looked sharply at the other two before clearly outlining the plan. "Number one, the campers are so deep in the woods they may not be aware of the danger. We must warn them—every second counts! Number two, the quicker the rangers know what's happening, the better. They will alert the fire station *pronto*, before hurrying over to help."

127

"Leave the campground to me," Geni answered breathlessly. "It'll be done *en un parpadeo de ojos,* in the blink of an eye."

"That's totally number one," Nick agreed, "and while you warn the campers, I'll rocket to the ranger headquarters and make such a racket that they'll chase after me if only to see why a raptor is behaving in such a crazy way. Luckily, the fire station is right next door. Then I'll come find you and Mike, but first, *rocket, racket, ranger.* I should be able to remember that!"

They both looked at Mike, who nodded his approval. "Go for it, good buddies! And while you're at it, speaking of *the blink of an eye,* there is another crucial detail that needs my immediate attention."

The eagle and the airborne teens flew in three different directions, parting glances expressing satisfaction with what they hoped to accomplish. The eagle often flashed Nick his "wise eagle" self-satisfied smile. But without a doubt, the boy realized that Mike Mulligan deserved a standing ovation today for spotting and responding to the fire emergency so quickly.

Nick soared up above the smoke and flames, partly to get a good look at the fire's progress, but also because he knew that the higher he flew, the faster he'd be able to dive toward Canyon Village. However, although it took only minutes to reach the ranger post, once he got there, the boy-raptor, still new to the job, wasn't sure what to do next to get the rangers' attention

He flapped twice around the building hoping to run into someone who he might persuade to help. Not a soul in sight. He was even prepared to fly through an open door or window if he could find one, but quickly realized they were all closed. Beginning to feel panicky, Nick circled around once more and this time spotted an open window he'd overlooked on the second floor.

In a flash he was inside zooming from room to room until, at last, he came upon a ranger, probably a member of the night crew, fast asleep on a cot. Knowing exactly what to do at that moment was no problem.

"Kweeaaaaah! Pi tip, pi tip, pi tip!" piped the hawk. The echo from his own screech was so piercing it caused Nick to veer off sharply in an unplanned maneuver, whacking his head on a light fixture that hung from the ceiling. But that was nothing compared to what the shriek did to the ranger. Still half asleep, he fell out of bed, leapt to his feet, and, looking for a quick exit, crashed headlong into the wall.

"Oh no," Nick thought, "how am I ever going to persuade him to follow me when he can't even find his way out of the room? Well, I know one thing—first I have to get him outside."

So off he flew, back out the window, landed on the porch near the front door, whacked a drumbeat on the wooden railing, and awaited further developments. Half a minute later, after the ranger had pulled on his boots and hat, he came bounding through the door at full speed. He skidded to a halt when he saw Nick the Hawk on the railing. That was the raptor's chance. He grabbed the hat off the ranger's head with his beak and shook it vigorously in front of the bewildered man's nose. Then he hovered over the ranger's pickup, dumped the hat in the truck bed, and perched on the hood.

Chapter 27—The Bear-proof Trash Can

As the ranger dashed toward the truck, Nick breathed a sigh of relief and thought, *Whew, I'm dealing with a savvy person.*

Jumping behind the wheel, the ranger started the engine and, with the hawk leading the way, understood that this crazy bird desperately wanted to be followed. Minutes later they rounded a corner, climbed a small hill where, from the top, one could see the smoke and flames billowing out of the forest on the far side of the Gibbon River valley. Just as quickly as they had gotten there, the ranger turned his truck around and sped back to the fire station. Nick watched until he was out of sight, then soared skyward in search of Geni.

Oddly enough, Nick heard her before he saw her. As the hawk-boy approached the campground from high in the sky, he imagined feeling the heat of the fire on his tail-feathers. *Or maybe,* he reasoned, *it's not my imagination!*

Visible above the treetops the flames, driven by the wind, were racing closer to the tents. As Nick plummeted toward the campground using his hawk eyes to spot Geni, he heard the unique sound—"Whee-ooo-quee, hoo-leee-lie-leee"—that she made when she became a loon. Suddenly, there she was, circling wildly overhead trying to turn the campers' attention toward the smoke and flame. As the campers recognized the peril, they shouted warnings to each other, grabbed whatever they could, jumped into their cars, and escaped to the safety of the village.

Joining Geni, Nick added his "Kweeaaaaah" warning to her loon call until the airborne rescue team believed that all the campers, totally alerted to the blaze, had left the campground. But as they flew near the parking area, they heard a dreadful cry. They spotted a woman sprinting frantically away from the cars and back toward the fire.

"Carrie, Carrie," she screamed. "Where are you?"

Glancing quickly at each other, Nick and Geni exchanged a look that required no words to understand.

The loon and the hawk dove together through the smoke and into the trees, circling every whichway above the flames, so low that the pair could feel the heat penetrating their feathers. But no Carrie. They were beginning to grow desperate until, all of a sudden, they saw something extremely peculiar. The lid on one of the special garbage cans, made to be bear-proof, was flapping up and down every few seconds.

"It might be," the same thought struck both of them, *"it just might be . . ."*

Down they dropped, right onto the lid, pried it open, and there inside was the best sight of their lives—a little red-haired girl hiding from the fire . . . *in a garbage can.* Although she was a mere *fledgling,* she was smart enough to realize that somehow the loon and the hawk were there to help her. She grabbed two pairs of bird legs and held on tight as they lifted off together to find her mother.

When the bird rescuers talked it over later, Geni would remember, "That child, Carrie, she was certainly brave, but oh my, *ella huele terrible,* she smelled awful from her time in the garbage can."

But when the frantic mother hugged her daughter tightly, with tears streaming down her cheeks, she didn't seem to notice the odor at all. She was so thankful and relieved that she totally ignored her daughter's strange arrival, hanging in midair beneath a plucky pair of the newly organized Yellowstone *flight-for-life team.*

At that very moment, sirens blaring, the ranger trucks and fire engines were rushing toward the burning trees. Hot, tired, and a little bit scorched, Nick and Geni settled at the edge of the Gibbon to drink deeply the cold, clear water.

A moment later, the loon gave the hawk a quick look and shouted, "Let's find Mike!"

Up they flew again, heading toward the meadow where they had last spotted the eagle, hoping to find him while there was still enough light to see. As they glided past the edge of the forest, the pair noticed a pine and spruce grove on fire. On they sped over the grassland, now black and smoldering, where herds of elk and bison had been grazing. When they reached the river, they came upon a memorable scene.

There, partly submerged, hundreds of the park's largest beasts stood in the middle of the stream. The water was up around the haunches of the adults, while the young ones held their heads just high enough to breathe. On the backs of many of the buffalo and elk, clinging for dear life, were the critters of Yellowstone—bobcats, lynx, coyotes, foxes, squirrels, rabbits, voles, chipmunks, weasels, badgers, skunks, minks, martens, ermines and muskrats, plus many that Nick and Geni couldn't identify. There were even three black bears, two grizzlies, a moose, and a wolverine paddling around in the water. Twenty or thirty more of the big guys still hesitated along the riverbank, while a dark object with white head and tail dive-bombed the slowpokes, hustling them into the safety of the stream. The dark

132

object was none other than *flight-for-life* leader Michael Mulligan, a dedicated *eagle scout* if ever there was one.

"Let's do it!" Nick yelled at Geni, as they shot down to help with the stragglers.

"*Estoy contigo*, I'm with you!" she repeated. Now the threesome joined in strike formation.

In what seemed only a twinkling, the remaining elk and bison moved obediently into the river, bewildered over where the Red Baron and his copilots had come from and exactly what they were doing. By then the campground had been evacuated and soon the fire would be under control. While the teens flew off to retrieve their backpacks and fishing gear, Mike did a brief eagle strut on the hilltop, a display of satisfaction over what had been accomplished. Then, recalling that he hadn't caught a trout for his dinner, and hungrier than ever from the exertion of the rescue operation, he rose into the sunset, squawking something that sounded like, "I'll catch mine before Nick's *Goofus Bug* or Geni's *Hot-Legs Hopper* even hit the water."

As the sun and the raptor disappeared together, the teens morphed back into fourteen year-olds in fishing outfits, both hoping to land a whopper bigger than Mike's. Nick hooked a pretty nice brown trout, while Geni pulled in a rainbow—slightly smaller the boy insisted, though she adamantly disagreed.

"Always suspected that you were a bit loony," Nick teased, "but now I'm positive."

They carried their prizes home, *rewards*, they winked at each other, for having played a major role in dealing with the fire. Mike Mulligan flew along overhead, a fat trout clutched in his claws.

133

"Nice work," said Mom, as Nick tried for the umpteenth time to teach Geni how to clean a fish. "As soon as Dad gets home, he will put them on the grill—then we'll invite Geni's mom and dad over for dinner on the porch."

When Nick's father arrived, the first thing he mentioned was the big news story of the day. "The rangers all agreed," concluding his description of the events surrounding the fire, "that never before have three birds—a bald eagle, a common loon, and a *Swainson's hawk*—warned the community of a forest fire, almost certainly saving both people and wildlife and preventing a disaster."

"Mmm, very interesting," said Nick, his curiosity aroused. "What else can you tell me about the Swainson's hawk?"

"An amazing bird," Dad replied. "It's a powerful flier that migrates farther than most—as far as 14,000 miles—from North America to Brazil and Argentina. Although it's mostly brown and white, you can recognize it by the reddish mark on its upper chest. Unlike most raptors, its preference to feed on locusts and hoppers has resulted in a snazzy second name—*the grasshopper hawk*."

At last, Nick knew what kind of hawk he had been. He glanced down at his own chest, then at Geni. The two teens winked at each other a second time, while the eagle, perched on the porch, was looking as if he knew it all.

The Animals' Christmas Dinner

Chapter 28—Winter in the Park

The two families loved summer in Yellowstone so much that both decided to spend Christmas vacation there. So they packed up a few presents that were easy to carry, loaded their cars, and traveled to the little year-round town on the north edge of the park called Mammoth Hot Springs.

There was so much snow that in some places the plows had cleared channels for the roads with walls eight feet high on one or both sides. Although it was wintry cold, Nick's family was well prepared. Before leaving home, they all bought heavy-duty mittens, insulated boots, hats that included earmuffs, down-filled parkas, and the coziest navy blue long-johns they could find. When they went outdoors, they may have looked like aliens from a frigid planet, but they were as warm and toasty as the bear family hibernating in its winter cave.

Imagine Nick's and Geni's pleasure when, a few hours after the girl's family arrived—Nick and his parents already there—they found each other having dinner in the Mammoth Hot Springs Lodge.

"*¡No lo puedo creer!*" Geni exclaimed. "I can't believe that we are all here for *la Navidad*." Then, flustered at having, for a moment, forgotten that Nick, now in Spanish III, could translate almost everything she said on his own. But her smile clearly announced that she was as excited to see him as he was to see her.

Later that evening, sitting near the roaring fire in the hotel lounge, Geni wanted to know what Nick had done in the days before her arrival and, in fact, he had remarkable news to share with her.

Ever since dinner, Nick had been bursting to tell her about an amazing scene he had come upon the day after they arrived. "It is so awesome," he declared, "I'll show you tomorrow rather than describe it tonight, okay?"

"*¡Eres impossible!*" she insisted. "*¡Dime immediatamente!* Or else!"

As Geni had correctly assumed, Nick's Spanish had improved over the past few months, partly because he was now in an advanced level at school. It was also due to lessons Geni had given him during the summer in exchange, when she could stand it, not only for his help in selecting the right dry-flies for fishing, but also, at her request, for sharing his knowledge of the stars and constellations in the night sky.

As for Nick, he was fully aware that once he hinted to her about something new and exciting, nothing would satisfy her prodigious curiosity except to spell out the details. With only token resistance, he gave in and began to tell the tale. Seven days before Christmas, bundled up against the cold, he had gone out early. The sun was shining, the snow was glistening white, the sky was perfect blue . . . and the temperature was seven below zero! Although the dawn of every day in Yellowstone filled him with anticipation, he never expected anything quite like what occurred.

He had walked up past the hot springs, impressed as always by the steam rising off the plateaus and the way the algae in the warm pools had produced shades of red, green, orange and brown on the terraces. A mile or so into the forest, much to his surprise, he came upon an opening in the center of which was a strange-looking grove of evergreen trees. It struck him as unusual because it was so different from the surrounding area.

Nick circled the grove looking for an entrance. After getting three-quarters of the way around, he figured it was just what it appeared to be—a thick grove of trees and nothing else.

"But, Geni," he said breathlessly, "a moment later I found a gap in the trees that I quickly stepped through. You can't imagine what I found! There I was, peering this way and that, standing in a large dome-shaped room. The trees formed sides like walls and came together at the top to create a rooftop almost two stories high. Inside it was quiet and warm, with enough light filtering through the upper branches to make everything visible. I thought I had discovered the best secret place I had ever seen."

"You make it seem magical," Geni agreed. "But is that all there was?"

"Just wait," Nick grinned. "Hold your breath to hear what happens next!"

Chapter 29—The Animals' Hidden Hollow

Eager to share the story with Geni, Nick began:

While I stood stock-still, looking into every nook and cranny of the grove, I was startled by a rustle in the opposite corner. I stared in the direction of the noise and spotted a movement in the wall of trees and bushes. In a moment, the intruder, a medium-sized black bear, crawled out from under a branch and checked out everything from wall to wall as if to determine whether anyone else was there. Realizing that the place was empty (I believe where I was standing I wasn't visible enough to be noticed), Blackie stomped over to a spot he had apparently selected, sat down and waited.

Only a minute later, two wolves entered together, possibly members of the Lamar Canyon pack that I knew from spending the day with them my first summer in the park. They growled greetings to the bear, who grunted once, then sat down along the far edge. A whitetail deer, the next to appear, seemed a little nervous because of the three predators, I supposed, but found herself an inconspicuous place to settle quietly. Then a mountain goat entered with a female golden eagle comfortably perched on its back. Neither paying much attention to the others, the pair ambled to the side opposite the entrance.

By now, I was really puzzled. What in the world was going on here? First a black bear followed by wolves, a whitetail doe, and a goat carrying an eagle on its back. While I was trying to figure all this out, two huge bison approached that, frankly, were really quite smelly. Moreover, they grabbed more than their share of the remaining space in the circle. Icy clots of snow that stuck to their mouths and noses caused steamy breath to rush noisily from their nostrils.

"*¡Espera un momento!*" Geni insisted. "Wait a minute! Are you trying to tell me that all these wild things entered *este lugar secreto*, this secret place, and didn't even notice that you were there?"

"I've thought about that ever since," Nick answered. "On the one hand, I was quite hidden by low-hanging branches; on the other, they were so intent on the reason for being there, perhaps they couldn't be bothered by a harmless human who stood silently watching from the sidelines. But then, *what was going on?* I was dying to know!"

During the next few minutes, a majestic bull moose strolled in grunting moose greetings, but otherwise paid little attention to anyone, including me. After the moose, several red foxes slithered through the bushes sniffing all around to catch any strange scents. Following the foxes, a cow elk leading a calf ducked under a low branch, paused to glance at the black bear, and filled an unclaimed spot in what was becoming a dreamlike vision. It began to dawn on me that the animals appeared to be gathering for a meeting.

A moment later, an American badger crawled in on short sturdy legs carrying a low-slung wide body. It glanced in a rather odd way at the foxes, but odder still at its newly arrived occasional enemy the coyote clan. Sometimes called "barking dogs," the coyote pups were making little yips and yaps as they huddled against their mother and stared wide-eyed at all the others.

Suddenly there was a loud crashing sound in the bushes and a violent shaking of branches, needles, and leaves as a hole opened and a huge form filled the gap. I assumed that everyone in that untamed place was trembling—at least I knew for sure that I was. In the next moment, the shape erupted through the opening and out sprang a massive grizzly bear stretching out his paws toward the ceiling and clawing the air as if to make sure everyone was aware of his great size. As he raised himself to his full height, a cascade of fresh snow fell from his back and shoulders completely burying an American red squirrel, much to its surprise.

I clapped hands over my eyes, but still sneaked a peek between my fingers to see the foxes and the coyotes all huddled together, the doe and goat pressed anxiously against each other.

139

"Are you sure you weren't having some kind of *sueño extraño?*" Geni interrupted.

Without answering, Nick continued:

The griz relaxed, found a comfortable pile of old leaves, and lay down on its back to do some serious scratching. I heard the animals breathe a sigh of relief, even the big guys who hadn't moved much since the mighty bear had arrived.

For a moment, I believed that all the creatures expected to attend this gathering had arrived . . . but I was wrong. Soundlessly, the last visitor appeared. As his head and pointed ears became visible, both bears and the moose leapt across the room and faced him as if to make it clear—"You are not welcome here!"

The mountain lion retreated into the bushes and lay down, resting his head on his paws. The lion's whiskers and brilliant yellow eyes remained visible as he peered out from under the lowest evergreen branches. Cautiously, the bears and the moose backed away to return to their original places. Finally, the circle seemed complete, even though I saw empty space around the mountain lion.

"What in the world happened then?" asked Geni, her imagination now captured by Nick's story.

"You are so right to wonder if I was having a *sueño extraño*," Nick answered, pleased he could easily translate the Spanish words for *weird dream* Geni had used a few minutes ago. "What I'd seen was hard to believe. I couldn't wait to find out what was going to happen next—and I didn't have long to wait."

Before I could blink twice, the moose moved sedately to the center of the circle. There the big guy stood wobbling his antlers, first to the left, then to the right, his glance encompassing the entire group. Seated quietly around the circle everyone respectfully paid attention to the moose.

"I still don't get how you could stand there up close without those wild creatures seeing you, or at least sniffing a human intruder close at hand. I think you were lucky," Geni continued, "not to have become *hora de comer*, at least for the canivores."

"OK, but chow-time or not, what happened next finally revealed something about why they were there—they were having an animal *round-circle discussion on some very special topic.* I couldn't understand what they were saying—at least until, thankfully, Mike Mulligan turned up."

Chapter 30—The Eagle's Color Commentary

"*¡No lo creo*! First you, second the animals, then Mike—what next!"

How he knew to find me there I'll never know. But all of a sudden, there he was. He nodded hello to the moose, seemed familiar with the bears, and gave the golden eagle a friendly wing-pat, all the while seriously ignoring the mountain lion. Then he leapt onto my shoulder whispering, "You'd be a little safer in here with the help of a magic berry, old buddy. But I'm proud of the courage it took for you to do it your way." Mike's arrival made me feel relieved from head to toe.

With my eagle-buddy there to explain what I couldn't understand made all the difference. First, I learned that no one spoke unless the moose gave the go-ahead. Second, no one ever interrupted, except once when the mountain goat tried to get a word in before the fox was finished and the moose whacked the goat across the flank with his left antler. And finally, Mike informed me, another animal get-together was in the works.

Whenever an animal had something to contribute, the others listened politely. The exchange continued for half an hour, maybe forty minutes, until, with virtually no disputes, the creatures reached agreement on a plan. Then, one after another exited through the gap in the wall of trees and disappeared into the forest. Not one, however, glanced at, much less came close to the lion on the way out. He remained partially hidden in the brush until everyone else had departed. Then he raised up, stared at me and Mike, yawned, twitched his tail, and left as silently as he had arrived.

"When I told Mike I wasn't sorry to see the lion go," Nick confessed to Geni, "he replied in an oddly thoughtful way. *You weren't the only one*, he said, *but don't decide about the cat of the mountain too quickly. It's too soon to draw conclusions.*"

"Following the amazing animal get-together," Nick continued telling Geni, "I trudged home through the snow. All evening and throughout the next few days I was unable to think of anything, even as Christmas day approached, except the assembly of wild things I witnessed like a fly on the wall. For several days I hiked back to the mystifying place several times, and hung around, hoping the animals would return—but they didn't."

"Based on what I had observed and learned from Mike Mulligan, I was able to draw several conclusions. The meeting had been planned in advance; all the animals were invited to attend, except the mountain lion; each animal even knew where in the circle it was supposed to sit; the moose was in charge; and every creature had something to say, except the *catamount* (one of the mountain lion's many names), who was almost invisible as he crouched in the bushes. By the time they adjourned, a second event was arranged, and some kind of agreement had been reached that pleased them all. But more than that I did not understand. Mike Mulligan chose to shed no additional light. In any case, certain that it all meant something special, I promised myself that the two of us would find out what."

As they said goodnight to each other, Geni observed, "Now that I'm here, maybe we can go to the grove together and figure out what is going on. After all, we are the #1 Yellowstone Park Detectives."

Christmas morning was sunny and beautiful, with a foot of new snow on the ground. Nick awoke early, peered outside, then went into the living room to see if Santa had visited. Soon Mom and Dad came in with their morning coffee, plus hot chocolate for Nick. The three of them sat around opening presents—a *camera, new binoculars, and nifty-looking snowshoes, perfect for winter in Yellowstone*, Nick thought;

scrumptious stuff like the malted milk balls in his stocking were great any time of year.

But as much as the boy liked his new things, he couldn't keep the strange encounter with the animals out of his mind. Right after lunch, he put on his boots and snowshoes, hat and gloves, and headed straight for Geni's door.

"*¡Feliz Navidad!*" she greeted him happily. "I have something for you."

"Merry Christmas to you, too," Nick chirped, handing her a small, flat package wrapped in red paper onto which dried yellow wildflowers had been arranged.

Eagerly she opened it, then became completely still as she gazed at the piece of writing, a poem, on a sheet of parchment paper encased in a frame carefully constructed from small aspen branches, bark, knots, and all.

"Oh Nick," Geni exclaimed as she turned all her attention to reading his verse, titled *Along the Lamar*. "I love it! It makes me all *emotivo*, reminding me of the *horas asombrosas,* the amazing hours we have spent along the Lamar. Now here is yours."

She reached behind the small wooden chest against the wall next to the fireplace on which stood a miniature Christmas tree, 14 inches high, and brought out another package, this one wrapped in plain brown paper. As he started to open it carefully, Nick caught a glimpse of what it was, paused, and removed all the remaining brown paper. It was a portrait of none other than Michael Mulligan, Esq., perched on the branch of a dead tree surveying the Lamar Valley.

Nick held it out in front of him. A huge smile filled his face and his eyes sparkled with pleasure. Elated by his reaction, Geni moved around next to him so that they could enjoy the painting together.

"Remember the day the Griz gave you a fishing lesson while I went to the watercolor class?"

"Of course I do," Nick easily recalled. "You described it as an excellent lesson except for the *bobo bald eagle* who insisted on posing for everyone's picture."

"Well, this is the result," she smiled, "and that, of course, is Señor Mulligan. Do you think I caught his image?"

"It's wonderful, Geni, and I know when he sees it he will think so, too."

After their gift exchange, the twosome started out across the fresh powder snow. In minutes, they were above the hot springs at the spot where Nick had first come upon the trail that led to the hidden hollow.

This time, he promised himself, *we're going to hang around as long as it takes to solve the mystery.*

But before they entered the forest, they were joined by the raptor who had been such an important part of their lives for the last two summers.

"Ready for the animal get-together?" Mike Mulligan inquired.

"You bet we are!" Nick answered emphatically.

145

"*Tal vez sí, tal vez no,*" was Geni's *maybe yes, maybe no* reply.

"Did you remember to bring the magic berries this time?" the eagle wanted to know.

"You bet we did!" came the affirmative answer.

"Well then, what are we waiting for?"

Chapter 31—The Snowshoe Hares' Christmas Surprise

The teens each swallowed a berry, pausing with anticipation, as they prepared for the magical change to take place. *It did not, however, turn out exactly as they expected.*

"We haven't been a Pronghorn Antelope yet," Nick observed, "maybe now."

"Haven't been a Long-tailed Weasel either," Geni noted. "I've heard they are good hunters."

"But what if we become a Yellow-bellied Marmot?"

"Or a Bushy-tailed Woodrat?"

"Uh-oh," Nick protested, "the Golden Eagle would swoop up a woodrat in a buff-brown flash and a burst of gold."

Then, in the same moment, both teens began to change. Their bodies, soon covered in soft white fur, shrank to about fifteen inches in height; black tufts defined the edges of their ears. But most noticeable were their two hind feet, size 17 and well-padded, perfect as snowshoes for leaping, hopping, and bounding through deep powder. They had become a pair of Snowshoe Hares dressed in their winter white outfits.

"Must be a mistake," Mike Mulligan casually remarked. "You were supposed to be Rocky Mountain Bighorn Sheep. But it's okay. You're about the cutest pair of snow bunnies I've seen this winter up here in Mammoth Hot Springs."

"Just a minute, *pelota de goofy*, you goofball, what if a Canada Lynx comes to the gathering?" asked Geni.

"Hmm, yes, that could pose a problem. Sounds as if somehow you learned that the lynx population rises and falls depending on the availability of snowshoe hares for food. But not to worry, the local *lynx kindle*, family that is, is celebrating the holiday with relatives in the North Absaroka Wilderness."

Geni had had enough. "Señor Mulligan! You did this on purpose, you *ave-cerebro listo*, you clever bird-brain!"

"Just improving your flair for *dashing-thru-the-snow*, while adding a bit of merriment to the season," the eagle explained sweetly. "Now let's *hoppedy-hop* inside and get good seats before the crowd arrives," he suggested, quickly settling on a branch just above the hares.

When Nick and Geni later recalled the events of that Christmas Day, the first thing that came to mind was how quickly everything happened. No sooner had the *husk of hares*—the teenagers themselves—entered the secret room and settled in a spot where they hoped to go unnoticed, when the activity began in earnest.

The wolves scurried in carrying platters of something. In no time at all, the animals had entered with bundles in their arms or on their backs. Where a week before a species may have had only a single family representative, today it appeared that the entire household was there. The grizzly and black bear sloths roared in, each with two cubs. (In Yellowstone, it appears that bears don't hibernate until *after* the animals' Christmas dinner—but then who can say for sure?)

The coyote den and the colony of badgers arrived together, as did the skulk of foxes and the route of wolves. The white-tail doe tiptoed in with a buck and a fawn. The buck had a handsome rack and the fawn nuzzled against its mother's side. Waving a gracious wing at Mike Mulligan, the female golden eagle glided in alone. The mountain goat brought its relatives, the largest group of all, more numerous than the herd of *fragrant* bison that arrived panting louder than ever. Finally, the gang of elk and the moose clan entered, their arrival seeming to confirm that all the guests were there. *But it was not so.*

Just as the animals began to open their bundles, there was a commotion at the entrance that caused everyone to stop and stare in that direction. In the doorway stood the mountain lion . . . with the mother lion and the two cutest, best-behaved cubs anyone had ever seen. Each of them was carrying a lovely bouquet of wildflowers— Indian Paintbrush, Blue Columbine and lovely Rocky Mountain Fringed Gentian. But what especially startled the entire gathering was the fact that all four were smiling in such a friendly way, and purring so loudly it sounded like an echo bouncing off the walls of the secret room.

All the other animals looked intently at them, then at each other, then back at the lions. After a hushed moment, the moose-leader strode into the center of the circle and gave a thumbs up or thumbs down signal to the other animals. Then he nodded his head three times and on the third nod every single creature gave the thumbs up sign. (*No one seemed to care where the flowers came from in December or that most animals don't have thumbs.*)

Geni leaned over and whispered in Nick's ear, "I don't understand what just happened here."

In a hushed voice, Nick explained, "When a group wants to take a vote, one way of doing it is to have the leader announce that on the count of three you must hold your thumb up to say 'yes' or point it down to say 'no.' So the moose asked the animals to vote on whether the *lion pride* could stay and everybody voted yes."

"*¡Qué fantástico!*" Geni breathed, her eyes wide with pleasure. "They are so kind to each other even though *algunos tienen miedo.*"

"Yes," Nick quickly agreed, Spanish III translation kicking in, "*some of them are a little scared*, but don't forget, speaking of being nervous, here's a griz, there's a lion, and you're a snowshoe hare!"

Immediately following the vote, the two largest bears and the wolverine went over to welcome the lion family to the animals' holiday celebration. The fawn, however, looked a little nervous for a few minutes, but then started to frolic with one of the coyote pups and a young badger, while the lion cubs began to crawl all over the mountain goat and its relatives. Everything was going to be okay.

After placing the lions' wildflower bouquets right in the middle of the circle, one after another the animals presented and described the dishes they had prepared. The black bears brought wildberry jelly and the grizzly family honeycomb relish with prickly pear cactus muffins. Wanting to please the carnivores, the foxes had simmered a delectable critter stew for three days, and the coyotes, calling upon an old German recipe, had made varmint schnitzel— both dishes smelled stupendous. The wolves contributed carrion canapes in the shape of miniature antelopes, and the golden eagle provided a knockout trout pâté.

The badgers had prepared an organic cabbage slaw, and the deer a prairie grass omelet made with buzzard eggs. The moose and the bison had collaborated, the first bringing water-lily salsa preserved last September and the second spicy buffalo chips. The mountain goat relatives had produced what they referred to as hi-altitude cheese fondue to which the bison had generously offered additional chips for dipping. But when all was said and done, *almost* everyone agreed that the elk had won the master-chef award for aspen leaf roll-ups filled with juniper bark birds-nest crumbles.

When the dinner-bell rang and the feast commenced, the pair of newly minted snowshoe hares sat in astonishment as they listened to each animal share the recipe of the dish he or she had brought. They were relieved to learn that there was so much food no one ever asked them for their contribution to the feast.

At last, the teens knew the purpose of the animals' discussion here a week ago, what arrangements had been decided, and why they had returned to the secret grove on Christmas Day. Nick and Geni were thrilled to be present, even as snow-bunnies, at the animals' joyous Noel in Yellowstone Park. It was a special treat to hear them singing their own versions of Christmas carols: "Hark the Feral Coyotes Sing," "God Rest Ye Hairy Grizzly Bears," "What Cub Is This?" and, of course, the all-time Yuletide favorite, "Sheep May Safely Graze."

Before they became teen-agers again, the two snowshoe hares, *snowshoed* lightly over inches of fresh white powder toward home. Filled with a warm and happy glow, they kept an eye on their buddy who flew overhead. As he coasted above them, Mike Mulligan thought what a lucky eagle he was to live in such an exciting place and be able to share it with his two best friends.

A week later, as they sat on the deck enjoying New Year's Day in the warm sunshine, the three buddies went over the strange but amazing details of the *Animals' Christmas Dinner*.

"What did you like most?" Geni asked.

"The vote about the mountain lions," Nick decided, "although the whole thing was pretty amazing. How about you?"

"At first, I thought it was going to be one of your wild tales. But I was wrong—in truth, it was *la Navidad más impresionante,* the most awesome Christmas ever! And yes, I liked the vote best, too. But I can't make up my mind about second place between the uniquely Yellowstone menu and the yuletide carols. This has truly been a holiday *¡nunca, nunca olvidaremos!*"

"I will never ever forget either," Nick agreed, then turned to Mike Mulligan to ask, "Who gets your vote for the best dish, old buddy?"

"Señorita Golden Eagle's trout pâté, and please, no argument!" were the handsome bald eagle's final words on the subject.

About the Author

An English major in college and graduate school, I became not only a high school English teacher, but also a word-loving story-telling father of four and grandfather of eight. After teaching for twenty years, I spent the next two decades as the head of a PK12 college preparatory school. Continuing to teach and write throughout this time, I never distanced myself from the pleasure of the classroom. During those years and into retirement I read aloud, often my own stories, to lower and middle school classes.

After retiring, an ongoing writing project has been a series of stories set in Yellowstone Park, a place I have been drawn to many times ever since I was first mesmerized as a teenager. As groundwork, I studied the park's fauna and flora, fished its streams, and became a modestly accomplished photographer of its landscapes and living things.

Mike Mulligan, The Magic Eagle of Yellowstone, was published in April 2017. Written for 8–14-year-olds, it tells the story of two teenagers who befriend a young bald eagle. The eagle in turn provides, in captivating fictional terms, an opportunity for the boy and girl to experience and learn about the special wildness of the natural world to be found in Yellowstone Park. Along with scenes of action, the animals and the landscape are described in vivid detail.

When I first wrote these stories for my grandchildren, I was as yet unaware of how much pleasure they, and I, would derive from having Mike Mulligan in our lives. Sharing the love of Yellowstone's incomparable wildlife, wildflower filled landscapes, streams fashioned for the fly-fisherman, and the words carefully measured to describe them, led to a recognition of who I am and what I treasure.

Acknowledgements

The author wishes to acknowledge the meticulous level of support imparted by the editor, Marlene Blessing, whose thoughtful contributions improved every page; Hailey Dowling for the cover design and for managing the intricacies of the CreateSpace publishing process so successfully; David Beck, whose cover illustration beautifully introduced the stories' cast of characters; Art Davidson who, for the second time, provided a subtle awareness of how we can thrill to the recognition that we too are creatures of nature; and Marcia, whose partnership has touched, inspired and enhanced six decades of collaboration together.

And a final note: special thanks to Brenda Peterson, whose expertise not only impacted all of Book I, *Mike Mulligan, The Magic Eagle of Yellowstone*, but remained an active factor throughout the creation of Book II.

Made in the USA
Columbia, SC
09 December 2018